Toby had spent ten years dreaming Lia's dreams for her, making her every wish come true and seeing how she'd grown and changed. She'd become a woman before his blinkered eyes. And now she'd gone so far ahead of him he couldn't see her.

The title and tiara were the least of his problems. She loved him, wanted him—but she didn't *love* him, didn't *want* him. After half a lifetime of him being everything to her, she trusted him with the truth only now—when she believed it was too late.

But if Lia wanted a man to show her just how much he wanted her, he was the one to do it.

SUDDENLY
Royal!

A majestic new duet by Melissa James!

Meet Charlie and Lia Costa, an ordinary brother and sister who are about to discover they are SUDDENLY ROYAL!

Royally Crowned: Charlie and Lia take their rightful places on the throne of Hellenia.

Dutifully Betrothed: Royal protocol must be followed—two *suitable* matches have been arranged for the new king and princess....

Regally Wedded: But for convenience—or for love?

The unexpected king and princess of Hellenia must choose between their duty—and their hearts....

In April you met Charlie Costa, who went from rebel to king in a whirlwind!

This month meet his sister, Lia, who's just discovered she's a princess!

MELISSA JAMES

His Princess in the Making

SUDDENLY
Royal!

TORONTO • NEW YORK • LONDON
AMSTERDAM • PARIS • SYDNEY • HAMBURG
STOCKHOLM • ATHENS • TOKYO • MILAN • MADRID
PRAGUE • WARSAW • BUDAPEST • AUCKLAND

Recycling programs
for this product may
not exist in your area.

ISBN-13: 978-0-373-17591-8

HIS PRINCESS IN THE MAKING

First North American Publication 2009.

Printed in U.S.A.

Melissa James is a mother of three who lives in a beach suburb in New South Wales, Australia. A former nurse, waitress, shop assistant and perfume and chocolate demonstrator—among other things—she believes in taking on new jobs for the fun experience. She'll try anything at least once, to see what it feels like—a fact that scares her family on regular occasions. She fell into writing by accident when her husband brought home an article stating how much a famous romance author earned. She thought, *I can do that!* She can be found most mornings walking and swimming at her local beach with her husband, and every afternoon running around to her kids' sporting hobbies, while dreaming of flying, scuba diving, belaying down a cave or over a cliff—anywhere her characters are at the time!

Don't miss Melissa's next Harlequin Romance®
His Housekeeper Bride
October 2009

To an old friend who waited long years
for his damaged love to come to him.
I know the reward was worth the wait.

Thanks to Rachel, Robyn Grady and
Barbara Jeffcott-Geris for helping shape this book,
and special thanks to Barbara Daille-White
for an outsider's perspective.

PROLOGUE

Sydney clinic for eating disorders, ten years ago

"How is she today?"

The middle-aged specialist smiled up at the brown-skinned young giant hovering over him, with intense blue eyes filled with anxiety and stress. "I'd say you'd know the answer better than I do, Toby, since you stayed overnight and have spoken to her twice already today."

One side of the boy's mouth curved up in acknowledgement of the comment, but he said, "I meant to ask how her counselling session went."

The doctor reached up to lay a hand on the other's shoulder—a massive, muscled shoulder, evidence of his active profession. "Lia says what we want to hear, so we'll send her home. You know she only talks to you."

The doctor spoke without anger or frustration. Indeed, he'd never known a boy like this one. Not brother, not lover, but the most devoted friend any girl in this clinic had ever had. Here day and night for the girl he called "his best friend's sister," there were undercurrents that made everyone on staff smile.

But they never laughed. Not when the boy always knew what the near-silent girl wasn't saying, what she'd eat and when she'd eat—and when she needed a few hours in the outside world, going on a bushwalk or sitting on the beach.

Toby Winder was the most unorthodox support person everyone at the clinic had ever known. He'd read every book written on anorexia nervosa, and yet tossed out the rule books half the time, using his knowledge of Lia instead—and somehow his unique method of treatment worked. Lia was not only putting on weight, she was *happy*. She ate when he didn't coax her, but made her smile and laugh and feel cherished. He seemed to heal young Lia Costa just by being there, by knowing her as few family members or friends knew anyone with this secretive, killing disease.

Lia had lost so much in a year. First, her parents had died in a car crash. Within five months of their deaths she'd been rejected by the Australian Ballet because of her height. Now her grandmother had been diagnosed with breast cancer. It was enough to drive a girl as intense as Lia, with so little self-esteem, into starving herself.

Toby Winder was the single miracle keeping her alive. The biggest threat to recovery was feeling alone, ugly or unloved. He made her feel safe and beautiful and loved, made her feel special by calling her by her real name, Giulia, when everyone else called her Lia.

A first-year fireman, he'd managed to arrange his schedule to be the opposite to Lia's brother Charlie, a fellow fireman, so that if one of them couldn't be there the other could, or so her grandfather could visit Lia around his wife's visiting hours. Toby had asked them both to hide their anxiety, which only put an added burden on Lia. He'd shown them the parts of the garden she liked at the clinic, and the games she enjoyed playing, eating when she was so absorbed in the fun she barely noticed.

When he'd discovered that Lia exercised all night if left alone, still trying to lose the last vestiges of the slender yet curvaceous figure that she believed had kept her from the ballet, Toby had cajoled the staff into putting a camp-bed beside her at night. How he slept with his six-foot-five frame on that squeaky old bed, the staff never could work out. He simply said that if she was sleeping he could sleep.

And, when she needed to visit her ill grandmother, Toby took her—and by some miracle Lia never starved herself afterwards to deal with the stress, because Toby was there beside her.

Nobody on the staff had ever seen a case like this. They'd never seen an anorexic girl's face light up the way Lia's did when she saw Toby come through the gates, or when she heard his voice. Anorexic girls rarely welcomed touch the way she did with Toby. And *nobody* had seen a nineteen-year-old boy put aside his entire life to help someone who wasn't even his girlfriend to recover from this unrecoverable disease, giving and giving without a hope of reward apart from her return to health.

All of which made the doctor's task so much harder now.

"You've been incredibly devoted to her recovery," the doctor began gently. "We've all been amazed by the way she responds to you."

Toby reddened and shrugged a shoulder. "She's my friend."

"I think she's a little more than that to you…or a lot. Isn't she?" he pressed.

The boy turned towards the window. "I think I'll go find her."

"This is for her sake, Toby. I need to know."

Toby didn't turn back, but the way he rubbed his neck told the doctor he'd rather have him stick pins in him than answer these questions. "We've been friends for five years, since Charlie took me home to meet the family. She was only eleven. She was like one of my little sisters to me. I moved in with the family a year later." He didn't elaborate why, and Dr Evans realised Toby was as secretive as Lia.

"When did it change for you?" the doctor asked, gentle but remorseless.

A long silence followed. Then, slowly, he said, "When she came here. When she collapsed. I knew then."

"Knew?"

He frowned fiercely out of the window, as if something there offended him. "I'm going to marry her."

Five blunt words, but from the mouth of this boy, so young and yet so old beyond his years, they didn't seem romantic, melodramatic or ridiculous. It was a vow made all the stronger for the unemotional way he'd said it.

And that only made the doctor's task harder now. "You can't tell her."

Toby wheeled round. The doctor shrank from the unaccustomed ferocity in the boy's face. "Why not?"

And the doctor knew he'd chosen the right time. Toby *had* been about to show Lia the feelings he'd been bottling up for months during her recovery.

"Because you're her 'it' person. She needs your friendship to live."

"She'll always have it."

The doctor refused to step back this time, even when he saw Toby's massive fists clench—even as he imagined the rookie fireman breaking down burning walls and doors with a single punch. "Will she?"

"Yes." No protests, no outburst of teenage anger or indignation, and again his simplicity made him all the more believable.

"She can't be expected to make a decision of this calibre now, Toby. She's lost so much this year. That she's recovered to this point is a miracle in itself, and a testament to her inner strength and your devotion." Aching with pity, he forced himself to go on. "For the sake of her future health, you must take your cues from her. If she ever tells you she wants more than friendship, I'll be happy for you both."

"And if she doesn't?"

The rough pain in Toby's voice made the doctor's ache

even stronger. "Then you can't, either." He sighed, turning away; it hurt to look at him. "She needs you in a way I've never seen an anorexic patient need a single person before. Though everyone loves her, and she gives to everyone, you're the only one who knows her heart and soul. She trusts you to be there. If you ever withdrew the friendship, or broke her trust—"

"It won't happen."

"What if she doesn't feel the same way?" he asked quietly. "Will she still have your unswerving devotion when she brings home a boyfriend, a lover? Will you still give her everything she needs when she's sleeping with another man?"

For as long as he lived, Dr Evans would never forget the look on Toby Winder's face at that moment. Just the thought of Lia with another man turned this bronzed young giant pale and shaking, his eyes blank with devastation.

"She'll still have it," was all he said.

Many times in the past five months, the doctor had wished he'd known love the way this boy did. Now he was glad his heart was a little shallower.

"She's almost better now, but former anorexics need their trusted support systems through the greatest stresses in life— moving, death, weddings. Childbirth," he pressed. "If she married another man, but still needed your friendship, can you say with absolute certainty that you could devote yourself to her? Losing your friendship could send her back into anorexic behaviour patterns. The danger will always be there. Like alcoholics, they never completely recover. It's a stress release she'll always be tempted to return to. Intense stress, fear, loss or shock will lead to vomiting—and she'll remember the comfort of losing weight. It's a sense of control for her when the world spins out of control."

"I know all that," Toby said, his voice tight.

Hating this, Dr Evans added the final words to convince

him. "Even thinking she could lose your friendship might send her back here. Next time, it could kill her."

Toby's face whitened even more and his eyes darkened, but he didn't speak, didn't move. After a long wait, a single nod was all he gave in answer—but every line of the boy's body, the perspiration on his neck and forehead, told the doctor how very close to the edge he was.

Moved with pity, he reached out to touch his shoulder again, but Toby moved to the door. "She's coming."

He was out before the doctor could say another word.

The doctor moved to the window where Toby had been standing, and opened it.

The tall, slender girl, almost recovered now, was dressed in the anorexic 'uniform' of concealing trousers and a windcheater. She wandered the flowered paths, head down, with the listless, puppet-like attitude she always displayed until…

Toby walked towards Lia across the sunlit grass in the pretty, hilly gardens of the centre. When he came close, he spoke her name.

She looked up; her eyes lit. A smile was born, and filled her face until she was radiant. Her tumbled dark curls glistened in the sunlight. All the ethereal beauty lost inside her withdrawn nature when he wasn't near her came to life. *She* came to life.

The doctor shook his head in wonder. He wasn't an emotional man, but whenever he saw these two he thought of Juliet with Romeo, Isolde with Tristan.

Toby opened his arms and Lia ran into them.

A lump filled Dr Evans' throat. The joy on the boy's face as he held her, the serenity and completion on hers, almost convinced him he was doing the wrong thing. Could he throw out the rule book on love the way Toby had with healing her? Could he let them just *be?* Because the incandescence of this boy and girl when they were together was something he'd never seen before, and probably never would again.

But what if he was right? What if?

Despite her secretive nature, Lia had given some sweet memory, some piece of tender wisdom, to every person at the centre, staff or patient. She was one of those people everyone loved. From the first day Dr Evans had met Lia, every instinct had screamed at him that this girl *had* to live…and Toby Winder had made her want to live. He had to be there to catch her when she fell.

No, he couldn't risk Lia's life because a boy was in love now.

Yes, he'd done the right thing. But the doctor knew that he'd continue to question the wisdom of his decision until the day he died.

CHAPTER ONE

The present day

Austràlia's Newest Royals! Charlie and Lia Costa, the Boy and Girl from Ryde, Ready for Right Royal Marriages
  The Swan Lake Princess: From Giselle to Real-life Cinderella. Aussie Ballet Teacher Lia Costa Will Marry the Grand Duke of Falcandis! Date is Set...
  They're So In Love: Lia and Max Fall at First Sight. Will There Be A Double Wedding With Charlie and Jazmine?

As Toby tried to report for work at the fire station, he was crowded by a hundred eager faces and bodies pushing at him. The usual swarm of microphones was shoved in his face.

"Toby, how do you feel about your friends becoming royalty? Your mother told us that you feel left out."

"Will Charlie marry Princess Jazmine?"

"Is Lia in love with the Grand Duke?"

That's what I want to know. Toby couldn't answer the questions tossed at him, since neither Charlie nor Giulia had called him once, nor even written a note, since they'd disappeared a month ago. He *hated* that—though he was family, he wasn't family enough.

He cut the excited questions short with the weary, timeless,

"No comment." He pushed past the milling crowd of reporters into the fire station with the grim determination of a man used to the press.

He ought to be by now. Last year, he and Charlie had received more than enough of the star treatment after they'd saved some kids from a burning, collapsing house. But the past few days of intrusions, constant doorbell-ringing and phone calls at all hours had given him a gutful.

Since the story hit had world news four days ago, Toby had found he couldn't even attend a fire without being crowded and asked for his opinion on questions he couldn't answer. How the hell did stars handle this on a daily basis?

How had Charlie managed not to punch someone without his restraining influence? How was Giulia coping with the pressure? Was she eating? And, God help him, *did* she like that handsome Grand Duke? Had she fallen in love at a glance?

A disembodied voice filled the room via the loudspeaker. "Grizz, report to Leopard's office, stat."

Toby sighed and dropped down from the chin-up bar. Though they used the irreverent nicknames for each other—Toby's being "Grizzly Bear" because of his height and build—when you were called to the captain's office you didn't prevaricate.

He took the back stairs three at a time, hoping to God Leopard didn't have more questions about Charlie and Giulia, and ridiculous assertions that a fireman and a ballet teacher could be the lost heirs to a kingdom he'd only heard about on quiz shows. When he reached the office, two black-suited, unsmiling men turned to him, and he knew he was about to get answers at last. One said, "We need you to come with us now, sir, no questions asked."

It wasn't a request.

An hour later he landed in Canberra, at a quiet airfield reserved for VIPs.

For the next three hours he endured intense questioning, and instructions on what complete discretion really meant. Then, only then, was he introduced to Lady Eleni, a pretty, dark-haired woman who was personal assistant to Princess Jazmine—Charlie's fiancée. Then he was taken to a dressing room at the Hellenican Consulate in Canberra, where he changed from gym clothes to jeans and shirt from the suitcase packed for him by the Australian Security Intelligence Office. They'd thought of everything.

Including Lia's puppy, the excitable, scruffy Puck, who barked a series of excited yaps as they boarded the Hellenican royal jet.

She was shaking.

Standing in bright, late-summer sunshine outside the Summer Palace, wearing designer jeans and a lemon linen-shift and shoes that would have cost the same as her ballet school, Lia Costa waited for Toby to arrive.

But I'm not Lia Costa. I'm Giulia Maria Helena Marandis, Princess Royal-to-be, she reminded herself yet again, after a month of living in the Summer Palace in the small Mediterranean nation of Hellenia.

She reminded herself of it every day, almost every hour—and still she kept expecting the alarm to go off and to wake up back in her bedroom in Ryde…

Despite the day's warmth, her hands and feet were cold. She chewed on her lip as the black Rolls turned smoothly and came through the gates. She winced as the press took hundreds of shots of the car's occupants.

He was here. Toby was here.

The butterflies in her stomach turned to woodpeckers.

"It'll be fine, Lia, you'll see," Charlie muttered as he waited beside her. "Don't worry so much."

She smiled and pressed her brother's hand, knowing

Charlie didn't believe it any more than she did. Though he'd insisted on the King bringing Toby here, to talk everything out with their best friend, there was nothing anyone could say or do to fix the crisis she and Charlie found themselves in, unless they could find a way to turn back time. Charlie would be the next king of Hellenia, and Lia would be Princess Royal, with all its luxury—and its duty. Including creating much-needed royal heirs.

Charlie might be between a rock and a hard place, but at least he and Jazmine were deeply attracted. They had a chance at happiness.

She, Lia, had the choice of the devil and the stormy, blue sea.

The Rolls pulled up in front of them. The chauffeur opened the door for him and Toby, big, strong and dependable, emerged from the car. Joy surged through her at the sight of him.

Then she saw his face, let go of Charlie's hand and gasped. Something awful ran through her body, like she'd stuck her finger in an electrical socket.

Toby was her gentle giant, her quiet tower of strength, who knew and loved her just as she was despite her inadequacies. For more than a decade she'd counted on seeing the tenderness in his summer-sky eyes, the sweet curve of his slow, sunlit smile, and the flash of his deep-grooved dimples when he looked at her.

Now, as he took in the changes to her hair, the obvious designer touches to her clothes, the look on his face—cold and unemotional—hurt her. It had been so stupid to indulge in the small, pitiful hope that in these clothes, with her hair cut and some subtle make-up applied, he'd find her pretty at last…

Until this moment she'd never seen the blackness Charlie claimed was inside him. She had only one single memory where Toby had looked at her without a smile—the day she'd discovered his family was exploding, and she'd brought him home to live with the family. Even when she'd woken up in the clinic after her collapse four years later, he'd smiled, held her tight and thanked God she was still with him.

But today there was no smile. She saw his soul from the mirror of his eyes, turning the bright summer day to night. Until now she hadn't thought of his reaction to crossing the world for her, losing career, home and freedom of choice.

Lia fiddled with her hands. Her toes did the squirmy thing she hated. "T-Toby?"

His eyes met hers, in a searching that felt like a winter's night…and then, like a miracle unfolding before her, they softened and lightened.

"Toby," she whispered, and took a hesitant step. Her arms, of their own accord, reached for him. When his opened in return, and he smiled that slow, sunlit smile so uniquely his, she couldn't hold in the sob of relief.

"Toby, oh, Toby, I've missed you!" she choked, and ran slam into his arms.

"Giulia, beloved," he murmured into her hair as he held on fast.

And after a month of weathering storms of right royal proportions, the world felt right at last. Toby was here, her one-of-a-kind, wonderful friend who knew her, good and bad, weak or strong—and just loved her. She loved the endearments he used for her alone. Most women loved the way he spoke—or maybe they just loved his striking looks. But he'd never called the girls he'd dated "beloved," only her. She loved it—so different from "babe" or "doll" or "sweetheart", or the other normal nicknames guys called their women.

But she wasn't his woman—she never had been—and that made the difference. Friendly love took away demands, emotional confrontations and expectation.

She ought to know. After enduring the world's most stupid crush on her best friend all through her teen years, she'd finally given up hoping he'd look her way. Only then had the world shifted onto its right axis, and the best-friend love they were always meant to share had been theirs. They could hold each other without any silliness.

Only, the funny thing now was… Was he—*aroused?* No, that was ridiculous; he'd never wanted her that way. She tried to dismiss it from her mind as a guy thing, an involuntary reaction of some kind, and held tight to him anyway—best friends could do that. She whispered, "Toby, Toby," as if he was a phantom that might disappear at any moment.

He smiled down at her, tender and loving. "Miss me, beautiful girl?"

"Like half of me was gone," she choked. *Like the sunshine had disappeared.*

"So I gather I need not bow and say Your Highness, as instructed?"

The tone of his deep, rumbling voice, rich with teasing, made her gasp with relief. "You do and I'll hit you."

As he chuckled and caressed her hair, she kissed his cheek—and felt the old urge to taste his skin with her tongue.

Okay, so she'd never quite conquered this—this idiotic feeling of being turned on by her best friend. She'd accepted it couldn't happen. It was just a physical thing—probably because she'd never met another man who made her feel dainty, feminine and aroused with a touch. But she'd sworn long ago she'd never embarrass him, or herself, by burdening him with her desires again. She'd done that eleven years ago, at that wretched New Year's party, and had almost destroyed their friendship.

She'd never risk losing him again.

He'd given her so much during the past ten years. He'd just proved his devotion by crossing the world for her. Why ruin something so perfect and wonderful for something only one of them had ever wanted?

"Hey, Grizz, don't I even get a hello?"

Toby smiled at Charlie, but didn't let go of her. Possibly because he could tell she'd refuse to release him an inch. "Rip, my old friend—or must I call you Your Royal Highness now?"

"Oh, shut up, you dumb jerk," Charlie growled with a grin, and thumped him on the back. "Man, it's good to see you."

Lia pulled back to look into his eyes, the anxiety not quite dissipated. "You understand why we couldn't tell you anything or call you, don't you, Toby?"

"No, I don't understand in the least. I shall demand at least four home-made moussakas and two chocolate cakes in recompense for weeks of terror and loneliness without you, being followed by the press for my opinion on your status that I couldn't answer—not to mention feeding and being dragged on a leash down city streets and into trees and electrical poles by the abominable Puck. And let's not forget the 'no questions asked' abduction by ASIO, the interrogation and being whipped onto a jet without so much as a by-your-leave. You are permanently in my debt, beautiful girl—and I will demand adequate recompense at the appropriate time." He smiled down at her.

Stupid, stupid body... Why did she always quiver when he smiled like that? Why did a simple curve of his lips always make her feel as if the world had stopped and they were the only people in the universe? "I've been in your debt for years, and you've never once collected."

"Perhaps what I want needs a debt this massive, my Giulia," he said softly, with an intensity in his eyes she couldn't quite fathom. "Perhaps I always felt as deeply in your debt by your magnificent care for the tag-along in the family."

"Don't be silly, you *are* family. So where is Puck now?" she asked, hoping she didn't sound as breathless as she felt. If Toby knew what the sweet intimacy in his voice did to her, he'd... Well, no, he wouldn't laugh at her. Not again. But he'd be ashamed and embarrassed, and all the things he'd been before, making for months of unbearable awkwardness between them.

Toby cocked his head to the car with a long-suffering grin. "He wouldn't stop yapping and chasing his tail, even when they brought him to me. ASIO called in a veterinarian for clearance papers for him—and also, against my protests, for sedation. He should wake up any time now."

"Oh, my poor Puck!" She raced to the car, dragging Toby with her, and yanked the door open, her face splitting with a smile she hadn't felt inside herself since they'd walked into the lawyer's office in Sydney. Being Hellenia's Princess Royal was a privilege and honour; she knew that. But it was still alien to her. She felt as if she was stumbling though each long day of lessons and duties, working out ways to help the people of Hellenia, and brokering peace between Charlie and the King.

But now Toby was here, and all was right with the world.

"I can't believe you brought that mangy mongrel," Charlie grumbled good-naturedly as he followed them.

"Yes, a distinctly unroyal mutt—definitely not princess material. I dread seeing what antics he'll get up to in the palace. Giulia, perhaps it might be best to leave him in the travelling cage."

Lia ignored them both. They'd been mock-complaining about Puck since she'd brought him home as a puppy a year ago, a gift from one of her dance pupils. She'd originally called him Boofhead, but Toby had named him Puck—because, like the Shakespearean character, he annoyed everybody—and the name had stuck. She opened the travelling cage and pulled her sleepy dog out, half Miniature German Schnauzer and half heaven knew what. She lifted him against her chest and hugged him one-armed, because, even cuddling her pet, she couldn't let go of Toby, could hardly believe he was here. The nightmare felt more bearable with him beside her.

"Remember, you owe me four moussakas," he whispered

in her ear. "Among other debts I choose to collect at the right time and place."

Oh, how she loved and hated the warm, shivering excitement that streaked through her at the intimacy. Hated the sense of cheated unfairness that, of all the men in the world, only her dearest friend made her feel as if she was melting inside with a simple whisper.

Stop it. He's your best friend, almost a brother. You're a woman now, and a princess. You're practically engaged—to a rich, handsome, kind…stranger.

"Does your silence indicate that you're too grand these days to enter a kitchen to make me moussaka, Giulia?"

It took a mammoth effort to grin up at Toby as if nothing was wrong, but she'd been practising the skill for years, and she had the hang of it now. "No, the kitchen's too grand for me. You should see the one here. I went in one night, took one look and bolted back to my rooms."

His eyes twinkled. "You require my reassuring and close-to-massive presence to terminate the feeling of smallness in the royal scale of size, my Giulia?"

She choked on laughter. "You've got to know how much I've missed you, when hearing your crazy vocabulary makes me feel so happy."

He grinned, unperturbed by the teasing. "It all feels a little surreal to you still? I gather my presence makes things more real for you?"

Her eyes drank him in, her oasis in this sumptuous desert called royal life. "Nothing's right without you—or Puck," she added, to keep things light, holding tight to the mutt who rarely slowed down long enough for cuddles of this kind.

"Is that so?" Toby's grin seemed deliberately light, as if he was testing her. "You would appreciate my presence and blessing on your upcoming nuptials to the Grand Duke, Your Highness?"

She shivered. "Don't call me that," she whispered, resisting the urge to bury her face in his shoulder; instead she looked away. "I'm not her, I'm not that person…not with you. And—and Max…I…"

After a brief hesitation, he asked softly, "You don't like the Grand Duke?"

She saw Charlie's hand gripping his shoulder, and knew he wanted to know her answer too. They all wanted to know—the King, Jazmine, Charlie, her minders and diplomatic staff—not to mention the world press. Max was the only one who seemed willing to wait.

Well, they'd all have to wait. She had enough changes to deal with, just getting used to being called Your Highness, learning new duties and languages, and how to speak to strangers of varying importance with grace instead of blushing and wanting to hide. In being Hellenia's new princess, she finally felt as if she was in a position to help others, but she'd spent a quiet, almost invisible life until now. She didn't know how she'd accustom herself to being important to anyone, always being followed around, having black-suited, armed professionals watching her every move.

When it came to dissecting her emotions, she'd always felt like a fish on the end of a line, floundering about with no result. In all her life, it had seemed she could never have the few things she wanted, and could always have what she didn't want.

Max was the perfect, handsome, kind point in question.

"I do like Max. Of course I do," she said quietly. "He's lovely and kind, and understanding—handsome too." She flashed Toby a quirky grin. "He's the standard fairy-tale prince…well, duke. I do like him—everybody likes Max—but…" She stopped when she heard the stilted tone in her voice.

She'd long ago accepted that she was the kind of woman who cooked and cleaned and looked after others, not the kind men fell for—but it didn't stop the useless wishing. Why couldn't just *one* man look at her, really see her, and find her pretty—and to mean it, to *want* her?

And Max—didn't. In the month he'd become a friend, a willing listener and shoulder when this life overwhelmed her. It was brother-to-sister caring—again.

How could she tell Toby how humiliating it felt never to know how it felt to have a man want her? Especially when *he'd* been the man she'd wanted for so long, and he knew it. It could only fill him with embarrassment and guilt, when he'd never wanted her either.

The flashes of the cameras at the gates were still going a mile a second—and after looking over there Charlie's hand fell from Toby's shoulder. "I think it's time you went inside to meet the new rellies." There was dry humour in his tone.

"Including the little woman," Toby joked back, with a grin. Despite the endless stress of the past weeks, Lia wanted to smile. Toby always opened the door to Charlie's reluctant emotions with laughter, giving him time to gather his thoughts before he spoke.

"Little, but she makes an impact," Charlie shot back dryly, the grin diluted by the lifted brow. He turned toward the palace, his arm slung casually around Toby's shoulders. She held onto him from the other side.

It felt unbreakable: the Three Musketeers going into battle.

Four Musketeers, including Puck. The image of her tousled, yapping pet as D'Artagnan made her chuckle.

He didn't ask why she laughed. He knew she'd tell him.

She turned to Toby, biting a corner of her lip, filled with delicious laughter. "I wonder how the King's going to react to my dog in the palace."

"Vesuvius or Etna?" His tone was dry. "I've been informed His Majesty is somewhat of a hothead."

"Just a bit," Charlie answered, with a world of dryness in his voice.

"He's used to getting his way, that's for sure. And when he doesn't…" Lia shuddered. "With Theo Angelis and Puck in one room, I have a feeling the explosion will be more like Krakatoa."

CHAPTER TWO

OF COURSE, taking the dumb mutt out of the travelling cage ended in disaster.

Puck woke up just as Toby was connecting quite nicely with the bed-ridden old monarch. Puck squirmed out of Giulia's arms—*the stupid dog didn't know his luck resting against her beautiful breasts; if she ever let him that close he'd never move again*—and raced around the invalid's room, marking his territory with excited yelps.

Not the best introduction to the last member of the Costa family.

While servants flooded the place and everyone ran around after the dog—trying to stop the million-and-one leg-liftings Puck had to perform every time he was somewhere new—the King, the only one seemingly unperturbed by the canine antics, tipped his fingers in silent beckoning to Toby.

Toby crossed the room, knowing what was coming.

"Make no mistake, boy. You're here to talk them both into staying—to doing their duty to their country—and after the weddings you go back to where you belong," the King muttered.

While Toby wasn't about to rouse the fears of an old man recovering from a heart attack, no matter how minor, he couldn't lie either. "I came to help, sire—but I belong with Charlie and Giulia, no matter where they are. We're family, sire."

The simple statement of fact created his first enemy in the palace.

His own stupidity created the second.

When he met Princess Jazmine and the Grand Duke, he kept his attention on them. If his heart sank at the suave, handsome, friendly perfection that was Giulia's "lovely" Max, he kept it to himself. He was too aware that the King was watching his every interaction with Giulia like a hawk.

In a month, everything had changed. The old king, sick and in the twilight days of his rule, still held the power over whether he stayed or was bundled back on that jet—and Charlie and Giulia needed him here.

Yet, despite her earlier joy at his arrival, Giulia seemed too quiet. She was looking at her feet, avoiding everyone's eyes. In spite of her perfect appearance, something was wrong inside her—and yes, as he'd feared, she *had* lost weight. The lovely ripe curves he loved so much were too slender for a woman of five-foot-ten. Her skin was paler than he liked, and her eyes didn't have the fresh sparkle she always had when she'd been out in the sun, communing with nature—another of her stress releases, along with cooking and reading.

He'd have to get her out there again. That was, if he could get rid of all the black-suited minders, cameras and royal watchers. If he could allay the old man's suspicions and gain his trust.

It wasn't going to happen. Sick and fighting for the good of his people, the King had seen straight through all Toby's defences that had been in place for a decade. *The King knew how he felt about Giulia.* The only person who knew his secret was the only enemy he'd ever made in his life, and the most powerful man in the country.

So he might as well be honest. Any chance to get her alone, and let her tell him what was going on with her.

"Giulia, my beloved, to put it without any overkill, even jet food sucks. I've missed both you and your cooking like hell the past weeks. Therefore, I opine, it's way past the time when we disappear to discover the royal kitchens and make some of your unbelievably delicious moussaka, and those decadent mud muffins the way only you can make them…and we can talk."

Why did she take so long to look up? But when she did he lost his breath. For a moment, a bare second, as she lifted her gaze to his the look he'd hungered to see for a decade was there. The chocolate-dark, slumberous eyes held *desire*.

Then it vanished as if it had never been, leaving him wondering if it was jet lag, their long separation or the same useless wishing he'd known for so long.

But if he'd imagined it, so had Charlie and the King. Charlie's eyes were glazed with shock—and the look the old man gave Toby was even harder, more calculating. "I think it's time we allowed these three to catch up." The unspoken words hovered between king and commoner: *the sooner you help them decide, the sooner you go.*

As if in harmony with the King's silent declaration of war, Jazmine and Max both nodded. "We'll leave you," Max said, with a smile aimed at Giulia alone.

"No, we'll go to my room." Giulia sounded off-kilter. "No cameras."

"That wouldn't be appropriate for a princess, my dear," the King said, gently but with finality. "Even such an *old friend* as Toby cannot enter your room."

Watching closely, Toby saw her nostrils flare a little, her lush mouth tighten, but she nodded, a short, jerking movement of her head.

"I'll make sure the cameras are turned off in the tea room, and nobody will be at the balconies," Jazmine said quietly. "They can wait at the base of the stairs."

The King nodded, looking exhausted. "Well thought of, my dear." He waved them all out.

A minute later they'd entered some kind of sumptuous, gold-painted tea room, with antique furniture, and mirrors and paintings on the walls. It was beautiful but, to his mind, overdone. It screamed its importance unnecessarily. Whoever had commissioned this place had had a real ego problem.

After they'd made certain the cameras were turned off and the security detail was away from the outside doors, the Grand Duke—"call me Max"—said to Princess Jazmine, "I think it's time we leave them alone to talk." These Mediterranean women really had the most beautiful names.

Though it had been the right thing to say, the way he smiled at Giulia set Toby's teeth on edge. He spoke as if he knew Giulia, knew what she'd want and that he could give it to her. He smiled at her as if they were *close*.

What made it worse was the way Giulia smiled back.

Was it a friendly smile, or did it hold more? After a month, she'd given this man her trust, her friendship, and—no, *no*— her heart? Had she accepted the royal engagement after knowing the guy a few weeks, when he'd waited for her for ten long, agonising years?

A red haze clouded his vision. All the reasons for his silence vanished from his jet-lagged brain. For the first time in ten years he lost control, acting on impulse, obsession, years of love. "Wait."

Jazmine and Max turned back.

"Are the rumours true about the royal marriages for you— all four of you?" He stared hard at Max.

Taken aback by the directness of the attack, Max nodded. "It's the way things are done here. Though he's giving us all time, the King can enforce it by law if he feels it's in the best interests of the country."

"Then you need to know the true reason I'm here, besides advising my friends on what is best—not just for Hellenia, but for them."

And with that he snatched Giulia into his arms, bent her over his arm and kissed her…kissed her as he'd ached to do, body and soul, for a third of his life.

For the rest of his days he'd recall the feel of Giulia's lovely, supple dancer's body as he pulled her against him; the soft, full lips beneath his as he kissed her. Thank God—thank God—her hand fluttered up into his hair, she moulded herself against him and kissed him back for a brief, beautiful moment.

The gasps of everyone in the room awoke him to what he'd done.

Idiot! After ten years of patient waiting, he'd lost it in a moment. He'd kissed his intensely private Giulia in front of an audience.

But she'd kissed him back. *She'd kissed him.*

So he might as well be hanged for a sheep as a lamb. He met the Grand Duke's eyes without flinching or fear. "Whatever Charlie decides, I'll be doing my dead-level best to make Giulia choose to come home—with me. To become an ordinary firefighter's wife instead of making an arranged alliance with you for the sake of power and wealth." He stared at each of them in turn, keeping Giulia in the curve of his arm, loving the feel of her there, where she belonged. "Nobody knows how to care for her and cherish her as I do. She's mine."

Then, without a breath, he turned to her. It was Giulia's cue.

And the shock in her lovely eyes matched the stunned betrayal in her husky voice as she cried, "Toby, how *could* you?"

She tore herself from his arms and bolted from the room before he could react.

"Do you want company, Lia?"

From her favoured hidey-hole in the library—snuggling in corners with books had been her escape for years when the world felt out of control—Lia looked up with a smile at the woman who'd become a friend, a sister, within hours of meeting. "If it's you, Jazz." She patted the big, fat, curl-up-in-me leather reading-chair beside hers.

Jazmine kicked off her shoes and curled up with a sigh. "I love this room. I always have. What's that you're reading?"

Because Jazmine didn't pry, Lia wanted to tell her. "What's wrong with me? Why does everyone treat me like a child in need of protection?"

Jazmine's brows lifted, and Lia laughed, feeling weirdly relieved that her friend chose to laugh at her rather than cover for her. "Okay, everyone but you."

Jazmine shrugged. "I think it's a man thing. Men like to believe they're in control, and they hate change."

"Oh, right," Lia mocked, the fury back. "That explains what he did? He might have been in control, but it was a change from his normal behaviour all right."

Jazmine grinned. "You seemed to like it, from what I could see."

"All right, so I liked it," she snapped, surprising even herself with the need to blurt it all out. "I'm almost twenty-seven years old and today was the first time a man kissed me! I wanted to be a woman for once. What's so wrong with that?"

Jazmine gaped—literally. "You've never been kissed before today?"

Her blush grew deeper. "Do you mind? It was humiliating enough to say once."

"Of course it was. I'm sorry, Lia." Jazmine leaned over and hugged her. "But you're so beautiful. Men should be lining up to kiss you."

The words resonated in her soul. *Beautiful...* Someone outside the direct family had actually said it to her: *You're so beautiful.*

For years she'd felt abnormal. She'd never even been asked on a date in her life. Sometimes she thought a man seemed interested—one or two had asked for her number—but when nothing had come of it she'd felt confused and ashamed, wondering what was wrong with her.

Even now, with a title and fifty-million euros, Theo Angelis had to arrange her marriage because she couldn't find a man of her own. Though he'd arranged Charlie and Jazmine's marriage, it was obvious by the way they could barely keep their eyes and hands off each other that their marriage would be...normal. But while she'd been willing to think about marrying Max at first, she'd soon realised that he was like every other man she knew: he saw her as a friend, a sister, someone to be *kind* to, to protect.

"Well, they're not," she answered Jazmine, curt and cold, but she couldn't help it. "I'm twenty-six years old, and no man has ever touched me."

"Until today," Jazmine replied softly, with meaning.

Without warning, Lia felt choking tears rush to her eyes. She'd acted like the sixteen-year-old with a hopeless crush on her best friend she'd once been, instead of the princess she must be. She'd had her dream for a moment, and she'd paid for it. With his next words, the dream had quietly fallen in splintered fragments at her feet.

No one knows how to care for her and cherish her as I do.

It was all about the past. Her best friend wanted to look after her.

"Yes," she agreed, with a bitterness she couldn't hide. "Until today."

Jazmine stared at her, and seemed about to say something. Then the door opened, and Lady Eleni came in, looking unusually harried. "Princess Jazmine! Princess Giulia!"

They jumped out of their chairs and strode round the bookshelf that hid them from view. "Yes, Eleni, what is it?" Jazmine asked, cool and in control.

Lia wished she had the knack of that.

"You're wanted in the press room, Your Highnesses," Lady Eleni said in a rush. "Lord Orakis is causing more trouble while the King is ill. The King wishes you both to handle this before the news reaches Prince Kyriacos."

"Of course, we'll come now." Jazmine took Lia's hand and they headed down together—but they both knew the time had come. They knew what Orakis wanted: power. And with his growing base of support he knew he could gain it legitimately through marriage to a princess.

And with Charlie here to marry Jazmine, there was only one single princess left.

That night

Lia headed down the wide hall to the library, desperately needing some time out.

She rubbed her forehead as she opened the door to the library, finally allowing the stress headache to take control. First Toby's bombshell kiss, then the press conference from hell, and then she'd sat through a dinner so awkward it had seemed none of them could stomach their food. Could this day become any worse?

"Giulia."

Toby's voice came from her favourite chair. She sighed, but kept walking. This had to come; it might as well complete the crazy day this had been. "You found my cubby hole." She came round the bookshelf to him.

Toby smiled at her, but it was dark, strained. "The task was far from arduous when we've lived together fourteen years. You cook, run, dance or read when you're stressed." He held out the book she'd left on the reading table. "I see some things haven't changed. You always loved your historical romances." He patted the chair beside him.

She found herself smiling as she sat. "What girl doesn't? We all dream of happy endings, a prince on—" She skidded to an awkward halt.

His laugh wasn't the shared, chummy thing it had always been; it held an edge of hardness, blackness. "Well, it seems some of us will have our dreams, doesn't it, Your Highness? And some of us will return home."

Her brain felt as if it was knocking against her skull. "Stop it," she burst out, squashing the childish urge to cover her ears. "I didn't ask for this to happen."

The look he gave her was, unbelievably, one of betrayal. As if she'd done this to him. "You're not exactly complaining, are you? During the conference Charlie looked at you, and you nodded. You've made your choice—Your Highness." He sketched a mocking bow with a hand and his head. "Is this enough respect, or should I genuflect, prostrate myself in front of your magnificence?"

Taken aback by the unaccustomed ferocity in him, she stared. This wasn't the Toby she knew, her dearest friend and confidante for so many years. "What did you want me to do, turn my back on my brother when he needs me, refuse to help a country torn by war? Should I go home and leave Charlie to rebuild the nation and face the threat of Orakis alone?"

"Let's not forget the tiara, the title and the fifty-odd-million euros with your name on them, Your Royal Highness." The words were hard, bitter.

"Yes, the fifty million was the clincher," she shot at him, her voice shaking. "Money's all I've ever cared about. That's why ten million's already spoken for—I've got a lot of designer dresses and shoes to buy. I've always wanted to be rich and famous—the way I've chased fame shows that, doesn't it?"

"I wouldn't know, Your Highness. Maybe this is your replacement for the Australian Ballet. Maybe wearing a tiara and fifty-thousand-dollar dresses, marrying a rich and handsome Grand Duke and having your face on all the glossies and postage stamps is all the compensation and revenge any woman could ever need. They'll wish they'd accepted you now, won't they?"

"If you don't know the answer to that, you never knew me at all." She got to her feet, her heart hurting more than her head at this point. "I'm leaving before we say things we'll both regret."

He muttered something beneath his breath. Then he blew out a frustrated sigh. "I'm not exactly stating my case to my best advantage—I know that—but all this has knocked me sideways, Giulia. I don't know what I'm supposed to do."

"Join the club." She started to shake her head, but it hurt too much. "I wake up every morning and think *I'm going to be in my bedroom at home in Ryde. This can't be my life.* Then I open my eyes and I'm still here."

He was silent for a moment or two. It stretched out. Then he said quietly, "Do you want to be home in Ryde?"

She stared at him. "How could you know me for so many years and not know?" She sighed and rubbed at the top of her head and over her temples.

"I should have known you'd have one of your headaches after everything you've been through today." He switched off the lamp at the table, and pushed the second chair to face his. "Come and sit. Put your feet up."

By force of long habit, and because the pain was making her dizzy, she sat on the chair, kicked off her shoes and put her feet in his lap. When he used his thumbs on her pressure points, she blew out a sigh. "Better than the best medication available."

He didn't laugh at the old joke, but kept up the pain-relief technique he'd given her for years. When her body slumped, indicating the pain was subsiding, he said, "You need to talk, Giulia. You only get headaches when you feel overburdened."

"You think?" But she was too relieved at the dissipation of pain for the sarcasm to hold weight. "I wonder why? This morning, before you arrived, the royal doctor confirmed that

Theo Angelis will never resume his official duties. So, after a few weeks of knowing who he is, Charlie's going to be the next King of Hellenia. He's not ready for it; he still doesn't want it. Thanks to Orakis making trouble with the people and the press, he's also officially engaged to Jazmine, but…"

"But our beloved brother blew it with his new fiancée within minutes." His thumbs lessened the pressure, began moving in softer circles. "He was overwhelmed by the questions thrown at him during the press conference, confused by all the sudden changes to his life, and he hurt Jazmine."

"And all I did was hide." She sighed. "I should have been there for him, for both of them. Theo Angelis asked me to step up, to do what I've been trained for, but when it all got too hard Charlie was the one who got it right."

"Don't blame yourself. Charlie's been trained to react in emergency. It was as much his firefighter's instincts that helped him today as the lessons in royal protocol."

"My job should have helped me handle the spotlight too."

Toby smiled. "I have no doubt you'll handle it soon enough. You can dance in a spotlight as Giselle or a swan princess—you've arranged concerts with fifty squabbling children—but facing a hundred yelling strangers as yourself was a shock to you. For Charlie and me, it's a different matter. We're ourselves when we wade into the fray." As his thumbs created miracles on her feet, his fingers caressed the sensitive skin beneath her ankles.

She wanted to answer him, but couldn't. Oh, what he was doing to her? "Hmm," she murmured, in pure, sweet relief.

Don't think about it. Wanting him goes nowhere but back to the years of hopeless love—no, lust—for my best friend…

But if I married him, as he said he wants, he'd be my husband; lust is acceptable. He'd make love to me…

Oh, the poor, pathetic fool: a kiss that lasted only moments and she was already back in over her head, wanting what she couldn't have, for far greater and deeper reasons than the one inescapable fact that he didn't truly want her.

"Do you think he knows he's crazy about her yet?"

His voice broke in on her thoughts, tumbling around in her head like day-old clothes in the dryer needing washing again to clear the old, stale smell of hopelessly lusting after the only man she'd ever truly wanted. She risked a soft laugh, and her head only hurt a little. "Not at all—he's in Costa denial. He'll hang onto it as long as he can. He still wants to go home, but we all know he won't."

"He'll work it out sooner or later." His fingers moved like butterfly wings up her ankles, to her calves, and she forgot everything but the delicate magic of his touch bringing her body to life.

"Hmm…" She moved a little, lost in the movement of his fingers.

Soft, circular motions to the back of her knees, more sensual than medical. "And you're officially a princess."

"Don't want to talk about it," she sighed. *Just touch me.*

"Why is this Orakis such a threat, Giulia? Why does everyone let him get away with his violent and publicity-grabbing antics? Why isn't anyone putting a stop to it?"

She gave another sigh, but not one of contentment. The back of her right eye throbbed. She sat up, severing the connection between them by putting her feet to the floor. She rubbed the bone beneath her brow, and said it because she knew he wouldn't stop until he knew what caused her stress.

"Because he'd be the king now if the people hadn't deposed his family a few centuries ago. He's a charismatic man, by all accounts—he has about twenty percent of the country under his sway—and he wants what his family lost. He can gain that through marriage to a princess. He and his followers will cause more strife if they don't get what they want. And now Jazmine's taken."

Even in the warm darkness, she saw his skin pale. "My God, Giulia."

She felt weary tears sting her eyes. "Orakis is unhappy about my possible engagement to Max. Theo Angelis has doubled Max's security, just in case, but if Orakis found out that you, a commoner, had any chance to marry a princess he'd lose it completely. He has spies in the palace..." She couldn't say more.

He pulled her hands into his, his thumbs on the pressure-point for headache—the webbing between thumb and index finger—rubbed in slow, firm circles on one hand and then the other. "How long have you been carrying this around?"

"Since yesterday morning." She bit her lip. "Charlie and Jazmine don't think I've made the connection yet, but now I've taken the title, as the law stands I have to marry either a Grand Duke—and Max is the only single one—or Orakis."

"What a mess." Toby swore, long and fluent and with all his inventiveness. "No wonder I was hijacked by ASIO."

She nodded, fighting tears of exhaustion. "When I realised the enormity of my decision—what it means for Hellenia, and for me—I just blanked out. I needed you." It felt like there was a jagged rock in her throat.

"And instead of lightening your burden I added to it with my wants and fears." His voice was filled with darkness, but turned inward, upon himself.

"I've put you in danger."

With a clear effort, he shook off the darkness and grinned. "Don't worry about me, beloved. After fighting the worst bush-fires on record as a volunteer, and running into collapsing buildings for a decade, a two-bit terrorist doesn't frighten me."

"You don't understand," she said quietly, feeling sad and lost. "You haven't been here to know what it's like, being a royal in a country that's seen so much war. It's not as the media portrays it. The reality beneath the glamour..." She rubbed her brow with her free hand. "A month ago, I was a simple ballet teacher. Now I'm this. The people have suffered so badly and I can help them, I *am* helping, but I don't know if I'm up to the task for life. But I've accepted the position, and it's all too much. There are so many strings to the position, I feel pulled every which way. I don't know what to do."

"Come here, beloved." His arms opened to her.

With a sigh of relief she went to him, and he gathered her onto his lap, caressing her hair. "I liked your hair longer," he whispered. "But you're still so beautiful."

Her head on his shoulder, she smiled. "That's my Toby, with all your nonsense compliments to make me laugh."

He stilled. "But you *are* beautiful, my Giulia."

"Don't," she whispered. "You can't fix this by saying nice things to me. I need you to be serious." She looked up at him, seeing his perplexed frown. "I can't talk to Charlie about this—he's under enough pressure about his own future. Theo Angelis is too sick to handle any dissention. He can't be the King any longer. His heart's failing and he wants everything tied up neatly before he dies. Theo Angelis needs me to do my duty. He believes even marrying Orakis is an honour if it brings peace to Hellenia. And Max…"

"Yes?" he asked quietly, when she didn't go on. "And Max?"

Her thoughts jumbled again, filled with sorrow, anger, regret and useless, hopeless wishing. "And he's like you."

Toby started and stared at her. "What?"

"He's like you." Sudden restlessness filled her. She jumped to her feet, pacing up and down the aisle. "He sees…"

"What does he see? Why is he me?"

She'd been silent or wise for the sake of others, hiding her true feelings for weeks. Now, with Toby here, she couldn't control the words bubbling from her mouth. "He doesn't see *me*. He sees the anorexic, and wants to help me—just like you." She gulped and breathed, trying to regain control. "If I ever get married I want my man to *adore* me, to want me so much he can't wait to touch me. Is it so much to ask, to have one man see me as a woman he can want and love?"

"Of course it's not, beloved," he said quietly. "You deserve all that and more."

She sighed and looked away from his intense, beautiful face, but said it bluntly. "I've always been a romantic—you know that—but now it's turned against me. I'm a twenty-six-year-old virgin. I can't *stand* the thought of my first time being with Orakis for political purposes, or a man who pities me." She felt a rush of hot bile rising in her throat. *Control, Lia. You will not revert to anorexic behaviour! You're stronger than that now.*

As she leaned against the bookshelf, warm, strong arms came round her, turning her to him, holding her against his body, so big and dependable and *perfect*. "I adore you, Giulia," he whispered. "I love touching you."

"I know you love me, but it's not the kind of love I want," she cried, struggling against him, beautiful temptation and dearest friend. "I'm not a child any more, Toby, I'm a *woman!* I'm sorry, but I'd almost rather face Orakis in the bedroom than a man who doesn't truly want me, who doesn't even think I'm pretty!"

He stilled. Completely. The moon, slanting in through a window, showed the stunned look on his face. "You think I don't find you pretty?"

She stared up at him. "Why wouldn't I? It's been right in front of me for years." Her hands pushed against him until he let go. "I know what I am, Toby." Suddenly she wanted to say it, even though she knew she wouldn't be able to look him in the eye tomorrow. "I'm the woman men see as their sister, the future aunt to their kids, everyone's dear friend who never gets married, never has a lover."

With the lightning-fast reflexes that made him such a magnificent firefighter, he had her back in his arms, plastered against him so fast she lost her breath. "How can you believe I'd cross the world for you, or tell you I want to marry you, from pity or fear? How could you not *know* how beautiful you are to me?"

Even with her body thudding and throbbing with desire from being near him, she laughed in disbelief. "How could I *think* it? How could I *not* think it? I'm nothing like the girls you've dated. I'm not blonde with a bubbly personality. I'm a tall, dark, quiet homebody. I do the bushwalking-and-kitchen scene, not the nightclub circuit. We've been friends fifteen years, and you've never once seen me, or showed a single sign of interest in me, until today."

His eyes burned into hers, pure blue fire. "I see you. I've always seen you."

"Yes," she said, filled with sadness. "I know you see me—but I also know *how* you see me. It took my becoming a princess to have you stop wrapping me in cotton wool. For ten years you've been wearing kid gloves with me. But I'm not your anorexic little sister—I'm a woman, Toby. *I'm a woman!* I can't marry you because you think you need to save me again. It would destroy both of us in the end."

When he didn't move or speak, she pulled away and walked back to the reading table. She picked up her book, and tried to speak as if nothing had happened. "I have another full day tomorrow. I need to sleep."

"This isn't over, Giulia." His voice was as dark as the shadows surrounding him.

"It never started to *be* over, Toby. I love you, but I won't marry you." She looked at him, her sorrow too great to hold in. "I know you want to keep me safe and happy. A few months ago I might have said yes—it might have been enough. But I can't go back. I have a life and responsibilities apart from one small ballet school and my brothers."

"I'm not your brother."

She shivered at the dark, lush tone, so inherently sexual, a tone she'd never heard from him until today. "Close enough." She sighed. "Toby, can we not do this? I have enough to cope with without more stress, more people wanting a piece of me. I've been trying so hard to keep the royal family together the past month, the one who stayed calm in the storm." A hiccup of distress broke from her. "But now it's official I—I need my best and dearest friend."

A quiet as deep as the night fell over them. When he spoke, he was gentle once again. "I made a vow ten years ago to be everything you need—and you need me now more than ever. I'm here, Giulia, for whatever you want of me."

How could she feel so relieved and so absurdly empty and annoyed all at once? *I don't need you to rescue me!* "Thank you." She turned to the door.

"I should have said *almost* whatever you want of me," he added, his voice soft but not gentle, and filled with a meaning that sent piercing desire shivering through her. "I am your friend, and I will be anything else you *want*." The slightest stress on the word *want* made her shiver again, right down to fingertips. "With one exception."

Oh, why had the stupid longings come back at a time when they'd never been more useless? She had a choice, neither of which involved what she wanted—unless she turned her back on a heritage that filled her with purpose and strength as much as it terrified her. She couldn't turn her back on a country and people that needed her.

But she couldn't stop herself from asking huskily, "What's that?"

His eyes held hers in a way she'd never seen before today. It was as if he'd taken the skin off his soul, showing her what lay inside. "I'm not your brother, Giulia. I won't be your brother."

"Why?" The word burst from her. "You've been—been almost…"

"Exactly—*almost*." His hand curved over her cheek, touching her as he'd always done, except that his eyes were no longer light or friendly, and a tiny moan escaped her. Her head fell back, drinking in the touch; she swayed into him. "We've never been brother and sister, even when we wanted to be. We've been best friends, we've lived together as family, but when we touch like this…" he trailed a finger down her throat, one unbearably perfect touch, and her body glowed and shimmered with the radiance of the desire she couldn't control "…we both know the truth."

"Toby," she whispered, aching, hurting, right down to her fingertips with the yearning for him, for *everything*.

"Say it, Giulia," he whispered back. "Say 'I want you, Toby,' and I'll be your friend and lover, tonight and every night."

His chest brushed oh so lightly against her breasts, and they swelled at the touch, blissful pain. She gasped.

"You don't know what you're asking of me." She ripped herself from his arms and bolted.

Toby froze in the warm, late-summer darkness, feeling it envelop him now she was gone. She'd taken the light and sweetness of hope with her, leaving him bruised, his body battered and in physical pain.

She didn't know.

Her blindness shocked him, her utter stone-blindness to his love. After ten years of showing her in every possible way how much he loved and wanted her, she didn't even think he found her pretty or interesting.

The doctor's words of years ago came back to haunt him.

No matter what you say or do, even you, her closest support person, may never know the depth of damage to her self-esteem or how she sees herself.

He leaned against the bookshelf where she'd been, inhaling

the last vestiges of her scent. How had he saved her life, been her best friend so many years, and known her so little? How had she listened to every word he'd said to her for so long, yet never truly grasped their meaning? She'd called his endearments "nonsense."

At this point, only one thing was clear: he'd shocked her to her core by kissing her today. She honestly hadn't seen it. She didn't even see how much he needed her.

If he wanted to win her, he couldn't take a single thing for granted. He had to start over from scratch, to show her he didn't just love her, he found her beautiful and desirable—the only woman he wanted.

I'm not a child any more, Toby; I'm a woman!

Ten years dreaming her dreams for her, making her every wish come true, and she'd grown and changed; she'd become a woman before his blinkered eyes. And now she'd gone so far ahead of him he couldn't see her. Worse, he hadn't even noticed when she'd left.

The title and tiara were the least of his problems. She loved him, wanted him, but she didn't *love* him, and didn't *want* him. After half a lifetime of being everything to her, she'd trusted him with the truth only now, when she believed it was too late.

How long had she been hiding this resentment from him? How long had she wanted a woman's life, and he hadn't noticed?

I'm a woman! The passionate lilt in her voice as she'd said it had both made him harder than he'd ever been, awakened him from ten years of aching love lost inside a mental fog of fear, and made him smile at last. So Max didn't see her as a woman? She wanted a man to *see* her, to want her as a woman?

As ever, half an hour with her inspired him. With two sentences, she'd shown him the way to opening her guarded and locked heart. She'd even shown him how he could stay in Hellenia, at least for now, how to circumvent the King's suspicions.

If Hellenia needed healing, he had some plans that just might impress the crusty old king.

And if Giulia wanted a man to show her just how much he wanted her, she was about to get it.

CHAPTER THREE

Two weeks later

"IT's a truly beautiful country. It's a shame so much of it has been torn to pieces by the warring factions," Toby said, sounding deeply thoughtful.

From beside him in the bullet-proof town car, Lia nodded. Every time she visited a new town or village shattered by the Orakis family's attempts to regain control, she wanted to cry. She felt so helpless, so inadequate to do all that was needed to help this beautiful, medieval country heal its scars.

How ridiculous was it that, by an accident of birth, the only choice Hellenia had for her next leader was a hereditary lord with the destructive tantrums of a two-year-old throwing his blocks, and two Australians who knew no more about ruling a nation than that spoiled baby? If it wasn't for Jazmine...

"Charlie's ideas are working very well—the village training system and paying for apprenticeships—and your charities and law repeals for widows, divorced women and orphans are making you a heroine in the nation."

Lia flushed. "I'm just doing what has to be done. Anyone would have done it."

"What, giving away a third of your fortune thus far to found refuges for women whose male family members are exploiting them? Using your second ancestral home in Malascos as an orphanage? I doubt five percent of the population would have done that." He added softly, "Papou and Yiayia would be proud of you."

Moved by the simple tribute, she smiled, glowing with the praise. She hadn't felt alone since he'd come here. She had her friend back…but not a brother.

She flushed and looked away at the thought. No, not even *almost* a brother.

"I see why you and Charlie feel needed here."

Attention arrested, she swung back to face him. He'd been silent on every other trip, unless she'd wanted to talk. He'd returned to being her best and supportive, wonderful friend… almost. And it was the "almost" that made her feel on edge. "Do you?"

As if he understood the turmoil creating storms inside her, he smiled. "Did you think I wouldn't? I've lived with you fourteen years, Giulia. I know your sense of duty, your need to help others if you can. I saw it long before you began volunteer work in the eating-disorder clinic."

She relaxed. Thank goodness, there were no undercurrents in that comment. But she found herself wondering why there weren't. "Yes, that's it. I feel like I'm finally where I'm meant to be."

"I can see that," he said softly. "Just because I want you in my arms, in my bed, doesn't mean I'm not still your best friend, and I'm not blind."

She stopped the gasp before it emerged, but his voice, the very air around them was filled with a dangerous, warm undertow that terrified her because it made her want so much. Want *him*.

He moved a finger, just one finger, just one millimetre, a tiny caress on the sensitive skin beneath her jaw—and she was lost to everything but the thick, heated pounding of her blood, the want. Her head fell back, only a tiny movement, but she knew and he knew. She couldn't speak, couldn't ask him to— couldn't tear her gaze from his, deep, shadowed face in the gathering dusk surrounding the car. The word was screaming in her mind but her mouth wouldn't work. *Why?*

As if he knew—of course he did—he answered, still filled with the rich, rumpled sensuality his gravelled voice could do so well. "You said you didn't believe my words, Giulia. So now I'm showing you what I want."

His finger moved again, trailing down the tender part of her throat. "Golden silk," he murmured, his gaze following his finger, and she shivered. "I've always wanted to touch it."

And she'd always wanted him to. She wanted that, and so much more. She wanted to curve her hand around his neck and into his dark-and-golden hair. She'd longed to run her fingers through the thick half curls for years, to see the desire in his summer-sky eyes as she touched him. She wanted to pull him down to her, to fall back on the butter-soft leather seating as they kissed. She wanted to feel him on her, feel him hard where she'd always wanted him to be for her…

It was so embarrassing, so humiliating that he could make her like this, lost inside her desires with a single touch, with no power to say a word, let alone "stop." Even worse that he knew it, had to know it.

"We're almost back at the palace." It was all he said, yet the quiver ran down her spine and into her toes, her core. He made it sound as if they stood at the door of a sumptuous hotel, or her bedroom.

When he lifted his hand from her skin, she wanted to cry out in protest.

"Can you speak to the King for me when we return? I think it's time for a family conclave on what's best for Hellenia. It's time to go forward."

Yanked from her sensuous daydream, she lifted her brows.

Theo Angelis had been icily civil to Toby since that first ten minutes after they'd met, making it clear that what Toby thought and felt about Hellenia was irrelevant.

This should prove to be interesting, to say the least.

"*Toby* wants to call a family conference?" Theo Angelis exploded. "By God, who does he think he is? The boy's gone too far this time!"

"An *informal* one, Theo Angelis, in the tea room. After dinner, if it suits you." Lia's lips twitched before returning to her customary gentleness with the King. She knew him well by now, he was so much like Papou, and Charlie for that matter. He needed the illusion of control to feel safe. It was a rare source of fun watching him trying to lock horns with Toby, who needed no such illusion, had no ego: he just saw what needed to be done and did it with a minimum of fuss.

"You might find what he has to say is interesting, Theo Angelis. He's been touring the cities and villages the past week with Charlie and Jazmine and I."

"You've been alone with him?" Theo Angelis growled.

It was a strain, but she smiled as she assured him, "I've been alone with him for years, and it's never been a problem."

"The boy's shown his hand. He wants to take you back with him."

It was more of a struggle for her to remain calm than she'd show, but she shrugged. "Of course he does. He's been estranged from his own family for a long time." She met the King's eyes. "He *is* our family, Theo Angelis, and if we care about Hellenia, so does he."

The King grunted, but his gaze was sharp on her. "He's going to do whatever it takes to make you return with him. Especially if you show a moment of weakness."

It was getting harder each day to remain wrapped in the shell of serenity she'd been using since she'd been in the clinic. Not only was the King suspicious, but spending time with Toby these days was like handling a live grenade. Without warning, he'd give her that look, that smile, and all her strong resolutions and good sense would vanish. Half the time he had to remind her what she'd been saying, or what he'd been saying.

And she spent far too much time wondering why he hadn't kissed her again.

"What time shall I tell him we'll meet?" she asked briskly.

"I'm not going to soothe you all. Hellenia's split in two—the Orakis and Marandis camps. The problem is, the ordinary people are the Marandis power base, and they're tired of fighting. The Orakis faction seems to thrive on it." Toby didn't bother to look around for reactions. "You all know this. What I'm saying is just a prelude. Charlie and Jazmine are clearly on track with what's needed. Their plans are helping villages and towns to be self-sufficient. Giulia's plans for widows, divorced women and orphans are falling into place." He smiled at Giulia, striving for friendliness, but knew he failed: his old self-control, once slipped, was like a broken mask he could no longer fit to his face.

"The last thing the nation needs is more war—but if Orakis doesn't get what he wants he'll bring it on. His people are more reactionary than those who love the Marandis royal family—or so it seems. So what the country needs is *defences*."

As one they all stared at him. He could see the doubt, the confusion in all eyes, except in Giulia's. The little smile told him she knew what he was going to say, and in her manner of quiet wisdom was willing to wait until last.

"You call a meeting to waste my time giving me unusable solutions?" The King leaned forward in the tapestry-covered wingback chair; his tea cup rattled as he thunked it down on the exquisitely carved chess-table. "I won't waste money set aside for roads, housing, hospitals and schools on guns!"

"No, Your Majesty, of course not. I'm talking about the *appearance* of defences." Still standing, as if he felt as much a supplicant as the old man wanted him to feel, Toby smiled at King Angelis. The King stared back, his rheumy eyes hard behind his glasses. "I've only been here two weeks. I'm an outsider, an Australian, and not a lord. I'm ignorant of the more important decisions in running a European nation. But Charlie will tell you that one of the first things we learn as firefighters is defence—how to protect ourselves and those we find in fires. And we learn how to teach people how to create defences for the future." He smiled at his oldest friend. "The same way we learned how to be firefighters before we applied, Charlie."

To his relief, Charlie nodded, grinning. "I see where you're going, but the logistics, convincing the treasury to release the funds, are going to be hard."

Giulia said softly, "They agreed to meet me cent for cent with the shelters. I think it's possible, if they're approached the right way."

The King turned to her. "Jazmine, Max and I would appreciate it if you all filled us in on what you already seem to know, Giulia."

He spoke in Hellenican Greek, a form of the old Koi. Trying to shut Toby out.

Toby had wondered when he'd try that.

Without missing a beat, Toby replied in the language Papou had taught him with painstaking care after he'd become an official part of the family. "I think if we present a proposal that saved as much money as possible, the treasury would be happy to cooperate. I'm talking about using retired experts—firefighters, builders, plumbers and the like. Teachers for the future, to teach your people how to rebuild the country their own way. Those who know the country best should be the ones to rebuild it."

The King's eyes narrowed, knowing he'd been outwitted.

Toby didn't smile, or acknowledge the win. He knew better than to meet fire with ice. Cool water was the trick here, and not splashed in the King's face. He was an old man who needed his dignity as his power failed.

"It's the same basic thought we have, sire—jobs, education, wealth. We teach locals to put out fires, to learn self-defence, to build strategic walls and clear land around villages and towns, so even planning attacks will be harder. Giving the village and townsfolk kids much-needed trades—stonemasonry and carpentry," Charlie said, with an excited grin. "We can give older tradespeople apprentices, and retired firefighters can teach people how to fireproof their homes to show Orakis that the towns and villages aren't as vulnerable as he thinks. We can mobilise the ordinary people for defence. They're used to running and hiding until the violence ends. This time they need something to take pride in, to fight for."

Giulia turned to Jazmine and the King, encompassing them both in her smile. "Charlie's right, Theo Angelis. So far we've been *re*active, not *pro*active. We're all working so hard to heal the hurts done by the war, but while it makes the people happy it leaves them passive—and gives Orakis the chance to destroy them again. We show him we're not putting plasters over the wounds he created, but equipping the people themselves to stand strong and choose the rulers who care enough to give them some power and say in their future."

Toby had been involved in family dynamics long enough to know when it was time to watch and wait in silence; but, ah, if he hadn't wanted to kiss Giulia before—and that had been basically all the time—right now he could have grabbed her and kissed her senseless in front of them all. Her quiet, well-chosen words reached down into the hearts of a royal family shattered by war, unable to see beyond the first tasks of healing. If Charlie had taken the bait and run with it, Giulia had given his practical proposal a Hellenican heart and soul.

The conversation took an excited turn. The King wanted to know how many people would participate in the scheme, how many they'd have to import from abroad. Max—whom Toby was beginning to like, despite his best efforts to hate his rival—said he'd go to the Duchy of Falcandis to find out. Charlie said he'd do the same in Malascos. The King told Jazmine to find out the mood of the rest of the nation on the idea, and Jazmine was smiling for the first time in weeks.

"When we have numbers we can go to the Treasury and call a meeting of the Hereditary House of Lords," the King said as Jazmine wheeled him out of the room, Max right behind them.

At the door, Charlie grinned at Toby. "Grizz, that was inspirational."

He grinned back and bowed. "I live to serve, Rip, my royal friend."

Charlie threw a paper clip at him. "I'm off to Malascos tonight. It's not like anyone needs me here at the moment. With His Majesty's forty-fifth celebrations in swing, I only seem to be in the way." He pulled a face. "I'll be back for the party, of course. I have to show my face, if nothing else is needed."

So things still weren't right between Charlie and Jazmine. He'd have to make time for Charlie soon. He'd hoped they could work it out if left alone. God knew he had his hands full trying to find a way to gain Giulia's trust. Without that, all the wanting in the world was useless.

"What can I do to help?"

Her soft voice, with the slightest touch of kitten-purring, made him realise they were alone. Did she know she only had that intimate touch to her when no one else was around? "You did it already." He looked over his shoulder at her with the smile he only ever gave her, the smile he only *felt* when he was with her. "You turned my thoughts to reality by convincing the King I'm something more than the man who wants to take you away. You showed him that I care about this place."

She took a step towards him, her face wise, lovely and so uncertain. "All I did was to show him the truth. Your plan was wonderful, Toby. *You* showed the King you care about Hellenia."

Her hair was tumbling to her shoulders, as she always had it when she was off the princess leash. Her eyes were locked on his mouth, deep, sleepy pools he wanted to lie down in. Her sweet mouth trembled.

She wants me. And even though he'd known that truth for days, every time he saw it again his body ached and throbbed, and a streak of white-hot heat ran through him like jagged lightning. *She still wants me after all these years. I didn't destroy it...*

"Both are the truth, my Giulia. I do care about Hellenia— and I want you." He didn't move, but willed her closer with smile, eyes and heart. *Come to me, my beloved girl. Come to me and touch me.*

Her lush mouth parted. Her tongue ran over her top lip, slightly fuller than the bottom one; delicious. Edible. He'd ached to nibble on that lip for years.

Soon. Soon...

"Princess Giulia, the King would like to see you at your earliest convenience."

As if she'd awakened from a dream, she blinked, and her head snapped round to where her new PA, Lady Olga Kanakarides, had spoken. "I'll come now."

As she passed him, he willed himself to be still, to let her go. He had to wait, even though it felt like that was all he ever did.

His patience was rewarded this time. At the door, she turned and gave him a slumberous smile. The smile of a woman almost ready to understand that the man she was smiling for wanted her.

Then the smile faltered; she turned back to the world outside this room and the delicate magic of one moment in time faded as a star at sunrise.

Whatever secrets were inside her remained locked there. For now.

The Wedding of His Royal Highness, Crown Prince
Kyriacos to Her Royal Highness, Princess Jazmine

"I'd like to ask the bride and groom to take the floor for the traditional bridal waltz. Prince Kyriacos personally chose the song, and wishes to dedicate it to his bride." In his combined duties of best man and master of ceremonies, Toby smiled and made a sweeping motion with his hand. He had the knack of royal behaviour down pat, despite not having the bloodline. He seemed to fit in with the beautiful people of Europe with no apparent effort.

Did nothing faze him, ever?

Lia smiled as she watched her brother Charlie take his bride's hand and lead her to the dance floor. Beneath her outward serenity, though, her heart was beating hard and fast. As maid of honour, she naturally must waltz with the best man.

She'd be in his arms for the first time in weeks, since the first day he'd arrived.

Though he'd touched her and told her how much he wanted her, she didn't know what to believe; how could she believe it? So she hadn't touched him at all, apart from taking his arm back down the aisle four hours ago. And she hadn't been alone with him since that family conference in the tea room: Theo Angelis had made certain of it, and for once she'd been grateful for the King's interference.

Yet all the contrived avoidance in the world hadn't stopped her *thinking*. She couldn't stop reliving the bare few moments when she'd been in his arms, not as friend but lover, and she still felt his lips on hers.

Her entire body pounded with excitement whenever she thought about it. And tonight, even the King couldn't stop them touching.

"Shall we?" Before she was ready, a hand she knew as well as her own was in front of her, strong and bronzed as the rest of him.

"Of course." So excited she was afraid to look up, she rose to her feet.

Toby kept her hand in his as he led her to the dance floor, and took her in his arms, positioning her beautifully for the Viennese Waltz.

Nine years ago, Papou had thought it a good idea if she learned ballroom dancing, and had arranged for Toby to learn with her. Of course he'd come; she'd rarely gone anywhere without him back then. He'd always picked her up for dancing lessons once she'd finished with the kids.

She'd never have learned if he hadn't taken her. His being six-five to her five-ten, they fit well together—and at seventeen, shy, awkward and uncomfortable with her imperfect, still-recovering body, the thought of facing a stranger, touching someone she didn't know, had been a major issue.

Now, as a woman, touching Toby was the issue.

He danced with a grace rare in such a big man, and he had no problems with the exaggerated movements of the dance that embarrassed so many Aussie guys. He held her close, and guided her into dips and swirls, with the strong arms and back that was his firefighting legacy.

Not too close, but not close enough, and nowhere near far enough away.

She could feel the envious glances by the glittering array of women in the room. To be held by this big, tough brute of a man...

They didn't know the truth: that the tough exterior held a heart so big and giving, he'd saved her life. He'd moved in when his parents had divorced because he'd needed her family, but he hadn't run when they'd needed help nursing their dying Yiayia. He'd stayed when, lost in grief after Yiayia's death, none of them had known what to do, and Papou had lost interest in life. Toby had become the glue that held her family together when it had almost fallen apart.

"Are you going to talk to me, Giulia, or are you pretending I don't exist for the benefit of our watchers?"

Startled, she looked up at him with a tiny frown. "I didn't think you were in the mood for conversation."

"You're right, I'm not." Slowly he dipped her and brought her back up, close to his face. She saw the sensuous intent in his intense, sky-blue eyes as he growled, "I want to kiss you."

Heat flashed through her, a wave of colour filling her cheeks.

He whirled her out, again with a slowness that felt like a seduction. He brought her back to his taut, hot body, beautifully clad in a tuxedo that cost more than she'd earned in a year back home.

He looked magnificent. Like a prince on fire. Like a man with every right to touch a princess in front of three hundred important onlookers.

Trouble was, she felt like anything *but* a princess when he touched her.

"Can we talk about something…anything?" she murmured, when the tension, the *need,* in her was a thin thread about to snap.

He smiled down at her, warm, intimate. "I'm at your service, for whatever you need, my Giulia."

A quiver streaked through her body; liquid heat pooled through her, hearing the soft possessive: *my* Giulia. "We've never discussed how it all happened, that first day when Charlie and I found out who we are."

His face softened. "You sounded frightened on the phone."

And though she'd started the conversation, the strangest

flash of annoyance ran through her. She moistened her lip with her tongue over a smile in an attempt to cover it. "It was more of a life-changing shock than anything—and you know how Charlie reacts to shocks."

A dimple came into play as he smiled back; his eyes were warm, like summer at the beach. "He turned ballistic, I gather, and you were exhausting all reserves to keep him under containment?"

She laughed, relieved to be finding a friendly footing with him. "Something like that." Actually, it had been exhilarating, liberating in a way she couldn't explain. Coming here had changed more than her name. She'd found out what she was capable of on her own.

Another dip, but this time he kept it under strict terms of dancing, and she breathed a sigh of cheated relief. "It can't have been easy for you."

After thinking about it, she said, "It was good practice for what lay ahead. Charlie and Theo Angelis needed almost constant mediation at first." The funny thing was that here, for the first time, she'd felt truly *needed*. It had taken all her negotiating skills and learned wisdom to keep things under control between the King and her brother. Max, while pretending he was the gallant knight ready to help her, had been more of a charming lone wolf with a chip on his shoulder, and Jazmine had needed a friend, a sister, as she'd fallen in love with Charlie almost at a glance.

Lia had risen to the occasion far better than she'd have believed. Instead of being the one everyone worried about, now she was the one everyone turned to.

"Not all of it has been bad for Charlie, obviously. He and Jazmine seem to have worked things out."

She turned to look at her brother and laughed. Charlie was kissing Jazmine again. He had a bad habit of kissing her no matter where they were. "Yes, they have."

"I saw several pictures of him in the papers with Jazmine on the way over here. None of them exactly portrayed a reluctant prince."

Indulgent, so happy for her brother, she said, "It's not the position that made this work, it was the woman. I think he'd sacrifice anything for Jazmine."

"Yes." Toby's voice turned softer, but not gentle; it was hotter, lush, like a heavy night. "There are some things worth making sacrifices for. When she touches him and he touches her, when he holds her close and they kiss, it's beautiful to behold. That kind of love only comes once in a lifetime to each man and woman."

Lia gulped and tried to breathe, but that thick, deep thudding of her blood took over again. "Yes."

As other couples drifted onto the dance floor, Toby looked down at her, his rough-handsome, just-craggy face smiling, his head slightly tilted. "Are you feeling well, Giulia, beloved? You sound a bit on the croaky side."

Beloved.

Hearing it again for the first time in weeks, and the sensual way he said her name—*Yoolya*—she shivered. He felt it, she knew he did, because he pulled her a little closer. "The night air is a touch chilly for you?"

"I'm fine." The words were abrupt; she didn't know what to say to him, or how to say it. She didn't want him to fuss; not that he sounded concerned, exactly, more like...

"You sound—I hesitate to say it, but—a little angry, all of a sudden," he murmured close to her ear. The tender growl of his rough voice moved under her skin. "Care to discuss the whys and wherefores?"

He only used polysyllabic words when he felt in control. She wanted to hit him for doing this to her, for making her feel too warm, too close, too confused. Her head was spinning like the movement of the dance. "Stop it, Toby," she said when he reeled her back in to his body, again an inch too close.

"What would you like me to stop?" he asked, his voice rough, sexual, velvet over gravel, seducing her. "Tell me and it's done. I'm at your service, Your Highness, as I've always been."

"Don't call me that," she snapped, weak and craving. "I have enough people putting me at a distance without you doing it too."

He grinned down at her, a brow lifted. "Pardon me, Giulia. I thought you *wanted* to put me at a distance."

"Yes—no—oh, just *stop*," she whispered, anguished. "We're in public, and there are a hundred eyes on me. I'm too new at this. I have to be seen to be doing everything right. It's been frightening and lonely and—and, oh, hard enough here. I wanted you here with me, but you've changed." Hot colour flooded her face, and she didn't know how to go on.

"How have I changed?" he whispered back, his face so close the chocolate, minted breath caressed her skin, her lips.

She closed her eyes, barely noticing her hands had clenched, holding hard to his hand and shoulder. "You're—you keep acting as if—"

"As if…?" His hand at her back drew her to him, until the current of his warmth filled all the chilled, lonely places of the past few months, of feeling so alone.

"Why are you doing this?" She was weary of trying to work him out. "I don't understand. You never wanted me. I accepted that. I got over you. We're—friends."

"If you're alluding to that miserable New Year's Eve almost eleven years ago, I've spent more than ten years paying penance for it." His thumb slipped between their linked hands, caressing her palm, until the thrumming heat in her became pounding desire. "Ten years yearning to turn the clock back and change my response when you kissed me, to unsay what hurt you so badly you couldn't look me in the face for weeks. Wishing I hadn't been so damned scared that the only family I had left, the only family I wanted, would kick me out if I touched you. I made you pay the price for my fear."

Strangely, the first time they discussed the thing that had happened eleven years before—the kiss—didn't break the mood, but escalated it. She saw the girl she'd been, who'd spent the whole night in a corner gathering up the courage to go to him at midnight and kiss not his cheek but his lips…and when she had, he'd kissed her back for ten beautiful seconds. "But—but you laughed at me, asked me if I was drunk, and then walked off and kissed that girl."

"All that that piece of male denial accomplished was to awaken me to the truth," he muttered roughly. "I closed my eyes and saw your face. I touched her and felt you. When she talked to me I heard you whispering 'kiss me for New Year's,' turning your face as I went to kiss your cheek, and all I wanted was to kiss you again. Then the words I'd said replayed over in my head, and I wished to God I could unsay them. When I came home and you avoided me for days, I knew how much I'd hurt you, and hated myself for it. I was given a trust, to look out for you that night, and I couldn't break it. But you'll never know how much I wanted to."

She shook her head, aching, wishing. "Why are you telling me now? It's years too late for this conversation. I want my friend back."

"Is it? Do you?" The words were so soft she barely heard, so close they touched her soul. So like the Toby she'd always had with her; the boy who'd saved her life and the man who'd devoted a decade to their friendship. So like the man who'd lived and danced, cooked and worked beside her for so many years. So like…and so unlike. "Do you want my friendship, Giulia? Only that?"

Confusion; lovely, awful confusion. What *did* she want? "I…" She couldn't go on. And she couldn't help it: despite her elegant hairdo and the tiara, her head fell to his shoulder and snuggled into his neck as she'd always done. Not quite friend, definitely not little sister. It was the closest she'd come in eleven years to saying three words to her best friend.

I want you.

The unspoken resonance quivered into her and shimmered outward, until he heard the silent music inside her. He moved another inch closer, and a half-inch, until the material of her dress moved in soft-satin friction against his shirt. A gossamer cobweb of touch.

She turned her face until her mouth was near his ear, almost afraid to break the enchantment holding them both. But soon, too soon, the music would end and real life would intrude and shatter this lovely, spun-glass bubble. "Who are you?"

He turned his face to hers, as delicate as the movement of the dance. "You know who I am."

She shook her head, the tiny movement brushing her skin against his, cheek to cheek; a dreamy lassitude stole over her.

"You know me. I'm the man who has done anything, everything, for you. For you alone. Always for you." Slowly, with a sensuality she'd never known, he dipped her back from the waist, holding her hips against his. "You're so lovely," he whispered in her ear. "A silver-and-golden angel, your hair shimmering in the light. The prettiest woman in the room, and I want you so much I'm hurting with it."

She shivered; her hand, at his shoulder, slid round to his neck. She laid it there, but one finger moved by itself to find his hair in a tiny fingertip caress. "No," she whispered back, afraid. "You don't want me."

"I can't think about anything but this, but you." His hand, at her waist, moved: delicate, butterfly touches she felt burn through her dress to her skin. She gasped and swayed against him.

"Giulia." His voice was rough, commanding, taut. "Look at me."

Slow and dreamy, she pulled back, still half-afraid, the other half a strange mix of wonder and confidence. She looked up at him and saw the stars behind his face. He'd danced her out onto a balcony, and her starved heart sang, a night-whisper only he could hear.

His eyes blazed into her soul. His mouth made her ache.

"Those big, sleepy eyes, so beautiful, are telling me how much you want me. I drown in them every time I see you. Every time you've looked at me like this in the past eight weeks, you've made me so hard it hurts."

If he'd treated her like a child for too long, he was making up for it now. The words sent a thrill ripping through her body. And his mouth—oh, his mouth—so close in the autumn darkness...

Where was she? Who was she? This was a new world, where she danced in marble halls and on balconies under the stars, she wore silk and satin and a tiara, and she almost felt pretty enough for him. This night, this moment, duty and bloodlines didn't matter, only he and she existed...

A new world, where he finally cradled her hip-to-hip like a lover, and every pore and cell of her thrilled to the hardness of him.

With thrumming intent, he brought her up and she met him, face to face, mouth to mouth. "You're the only one who knows me. I'm the man who slept beside you when you needed me, who learned to dance because you wanted it."

"That's—that's what brothers do," she murmured. Another finger joined the first, tips glorying in the feel of his hair against them, like hot silk.

"Do they? Did Charlie?" he whispered back. His hand moved round to her back and pulled her in closer, a delicious millimetre or two, in a semblance of dancing that brushed his body against hers.

"Oh." She blinked, tilted her head, and a smile grew and grew. "No."

"Because he didn't yearn for the chance to hold you like this for a few hours every week," he breathed near her mouth, so close. "I did. I still do."

"Oh." Unbearable brightness flooded her heart, her awakening body. "You did?" Her thumb found the skin beneath his collar and caressed it, exquisitely intimate.

"I did. I do." His eyes closed as he dipped her—a prelude, a promise—and brought her back. "Every week I hoped like hell you'd touch me like you just did."

I wanted to; oh, how I wanted to. But she couldn't say it, couldn't show him, even now. To risk everything all over again…

"Touch me again, Giulia." Rough-edged, hot, his voice shivered into her deepest core. "Touch me, beautiful girl, just touch me."

The words, more raw and commanding than pleading, sent anguished, painful longing through her, her skin too sensitive to the touch… Her hand wound into his hair, her palm filled with softness, her fingers with his skin. Her eyes closed. *Ah…*

"This is me," he murmured into her ear, rough, hard and aching with need. "I'm the man who moved into your house to become a part of your family, but mostly because I couldn't stay away from you. You fascinate me endlessly with every word and movement. I've kissed you ten-thousand times in my dreams and loved you only with words, hoping like hell you'd understand, while I was aching to do this." He moved his hips against her, and she moaned and gasped, her eyes closing again with intense, aching beauty and excitement.

"I'm the man who's been waiting ten long years for you to move a single inch."

An inch? Her eyes fluttered open, heavy with agonised passion. She looked at him and saw only his mouth, an inch from hers.

He dipped her again, slowly and sensually, a prelude to the inevitable, the beautiful and wanted. "I've always been right here, waiting. Move that inch, Giulia," he whispered against her lips. "Come to me. Give me you. Just an inch."

Floating between lovely dream and invisible reality, she released his other hand, slid hers up past his shoulder, over his neck and into his hair, pulled him down with hands trembling with eagerness, and opened her mouth to him.

A kiss is just a kiss. No, no; it was everything…

Soft and clinging, it was everything she'd hoped for through years filled with and yet starved of his touch. Gentle, as unforgettable as the song that had been playing when they'd started dancing. Their bodies were still apart, still dancing a warm current of wanting; delicate caresses of breast to chest almost incidental to the movement of the music, lips slanting in barely-there kisses filled with tenderness. And it was Toby who was kissing her, her dearest, beloved Toby…

"Your Highness, the King wishes to speak to you at your earliest convenience."

She felt Toby move back, but still dazed, she didn't realise the words were directed towards her; all she wanted was to keep kissing him, touching him. She pulled him back to her and kissed him again, moaning softly.

"Princess Giulia!"

She blinked, remembering that the title "princess" applied to her. Slowly, she turned to the speaker—Jazmine's PA, Lady Eleni, stood at the open doorway of the balcony. Lia sighed. "Thank you, Eleni. Please tell him I'll come soon." With an irritable motion, she waved her away.

Eleni's brows lifted, indicating her surprise, but she backed away.

She drew in another breath and looked up at Toby. His mouth was twisted in rueful amusement. She almost got lost again, just looking at him. "As they say in the classics, I think we've been busted."

A laugh burst from her. "Well, forewarned is forearmed." Her brows lifted in quirky acceptance. "I think I'll be on the receiving end of Theo Angelis's displeasure for once."

"I'll be right beside you." He took her hands in his. "I wouldn't leave you to face this alone."

She shook her head. "He wouldn't appreciate you protecting me. Don't worry, I can handle it."

"I started this. It's my place to be there and receive his anger." He frowned and searched her face, and a flash of annoyance tore through her. He was looking for signs of weakness—that she needed him.

"I'm fine," she said as briefly as before, and released his hands. "This has far more levels than the personal."

"I know that." He spoke with no impatience, yet she felt it, felt his annoyance—and no wonder. He'd not only taken Charlie's dream for Hellenia and run with it while Charlie was learning how to be a king; he'd also begun implementing his own plans. In the past eight weeks Toby had recruited retired firefighters from Hellenia and Australia and begun a centralised training school based in the capital, Orakidis City, and in Mirapoulos, the major city in the Malascos region, Papou's birthplace. He'd fought fires and taught volunteers and families the best way to protect their homes, schools, hospitals and villages from the wildfires that had destroyed a full third of the country last summer—and from the sneak attacks by Orakis's followers. He was helping to make the country safe. The people cheered him wherever he went.

He spoke before she could think of anything conciliating

to say. "Hold onto that regal attitude you unleashed on Lady Eleni when you speak to the King." He drew a tender line down her cheek with a finger. "You need to stand as his equal, Giulia. He's abdicating in a couple of months. This is your choice."

Subduing another unprecedented flash of irritation, she forced a smile. "I know how to deal with Theo Angelis."

"Of course you do. I've seen you wrap the old man around your finger."

"But this is an enormous thing. No member of the royal family has ever…" Again, she stopped, unsure.

"Married the fourth child of divorced, lower-middle-class parents?" he asked softly, sensually, every other emotion gone but the wanting. "I did propose to you, Giulia, if in a backdoor fashion. I'll do so in a more romantic style as soon as I can finally have you alone. And I'll be fervently awaiting your response."

She frowned. "Why, Toby? Why here, why now? Why did you wait until now, when—?" She stopped, realising how enormous the choice was that loomed before her. How many lives would be affected?

"No, it's not too late," he murmured, touching his forehead to hers. "Charlie and Jazmine just changed the law once. It can happen again. And if not—" he shrugged "—we have two houses to choose from in Sydney. You have your school still, the substitute teacher is there until you decide to sell. I have my job. We'll never have the kind of riches you enjoy here, but you'll never have to go without, that I swear to you. Everything I am, everything I have, belongs to you. It always has and always will."

Sadness swamped her without warning or reason. Why, when he'd said everything right? He'd been romantic and strong, and he'd kissed her as if he'd meant it. Her first kiss had been everything she'd wanted it to be.

But it was the wrong time, wrong place, far too late. The chasm was there between them now, no matter how they tried to bridge it. And she didn't *believe* him.

"I have to go." She turned quickly, before he could see her emotion.

"Giulia, if you're worried that he'll upset you…"

She repressed a sigh. "Thank you." The needle-fine politeness she'd used on Eleni came out again. "I'm a woman, Toby. I don't need you to come running to rescue me any more. I haven't given you the right."

She opened the hand he'd taken, forcing him to drop it, and she walked over to the King without looking back.

CHAPTER FOUR

WHAT the hell just happened?

From a convenient corner where only the wedding party and royal family could sit, Toby watched Giulia as she spoke to the King.

I can handle him.

She certainly could. Within two minutes, the King's scowl lightened, not in relief but love. Her hands were in the old man's; she kissed his cheek with a genuine affection that had shocked Toby the first time he'd seen it. Giulia's affection was deep, but she'd always kept it for family. She was reserved with strangers; it was her way.

But within weeks of leaving Sydney, she spoke to strangers daily, helping them with their problems in her role as princess. She was the King's pet, Jazmine's friend and sister—and as for the handsome young Grand Duke with a castle and two-hundred million euros...

Giulia smiled for Max, laughed with him and talked to him in a way she'd only talked with him, Toby, before.

How had she changed so much? She'd become a princess in more ways than the obvious. And now, only five minutes after the most beautiful kiss of his life, he had the sinking feeling there was no going back.

The woman he'd loved for ten years had always been like a flower touched by frost: coming to warm, vibrant life only for him. Now she was blossoming on her own, and that scared the living daylights out of him. If she didn't need him, who was he? What life did he have without her in it?

But then he saw her serene expression change. She paled and, beneath the silver silk dress that made her look like a dark-haired, golden-skinned angel, her toes started the tap-tap thing. He could see the slight up-down motion of her hem. One of her few secretive signs of stress. He got to his feet.

A hand fell on his shoulder as he took the first step. "Grizz, we need to talk."

Toby forced a smile as he turned to his turbulent best friend. "You have your hands full with your bride, Rip. You don't need to bother with me tonight."

"Well, I wouldn't have if you'd toed the line." Charlie didn't have the thundercloud look Toby had expected: another sign of his friend's rapid growth from volatile fireman to king-in-waiting. "Jazmine's gone to talk to Lia."

A sense of doom fell on him, hard and fast. "Is the entire royal family in array against me?" he asked lightly.

Charlie swore. "Look, this is hard enough to say. This is my wedding night, and you're my brother. If you'd come to me five, six months ago and said you wanted to marry Lia I'd have been the happiest bloke in Ryde."

Seeing Charlie floundering, Toby supplied the rest of it for him. "But now you aren't the happiest Crown Prince in the palace."

Charlie said bluntly, "Lia can't renounce her position without the permission of the reigning king and the entire House of Hereditary Lords—and with only four of us to rebuild the dynasty there's no way they'll let her go."

Toby went cold. "Does Giulia know that?"

"*I* didn't know until Jazmine told me a few days ago." Charlie sighed. "The law is designed to tie royalty to the nation for life. That's why Papou had to disappear the way he did, and could never come back." Charlie's mouth tightened. "I trust you with her life, Grizz, you know that. But you can't take her home."

He stared his old friend down. "Then I'll stay with her." The thought of a life without Giulia in it was unbearable. She and Charlie were his family, had been ever since his parents had divorced with a bitterness that had torn the Winders apart. His parents had demanded full loyalty, that he live with one parent or the other. Unable to stand it, he'd opted out and chosen the Costas—and neither of them had forgiven him for the betrayal.

"You can't." Charlie's voice grew stressed. "The people won't accept you. This is a male-dominated society, and whoever marries Lia becomes a prince by default."

A cold shiver ran through him. He loved Giulia, he always would. But he was a fireman. He loved his life at home. To have the woman he loved, he'd have to become a prince, facing the media and the task of rebuilding Hellenia on a daily, hourly basis. It was a vision as ridiculous as it was impossible.

He'd come to Hellenia ready to save her, convinced she'd collapse under the stress of royal life; but all he'd seen in the past eight weeks had been her strength, her wisdom, courage and dignity. Since coming to Hellenia, she'd flourished.

So what was he doing? Trying to ruin her new life filled with challenges she revelled in, weaken her strength to re-find his place with her?

Charlie ran a hand through his hair. "When you planted the first kiss on her, I brought up the notion of her marriage at the next session of the House of Hereditary Lords. They almost started a revolution." He shrugged. "Changing the law to allow a queen to co-rule with me is the most change they'll allow this decade. They're old-fashioned and class-conscious. In their minds, if Max or Orakis don't get Lia, one of their sons does. Change happens at the speed of a tortoise."

Voice and body tight with fury, Toby said, "'Get' Giulia, Rip? Listen to yourself. For the past fifteen years you've been ready to tear apart any man who approached her. Now you'll hand her over to the highest bidder?"

"Don't misquote me." Charlie's voice turned icy. "I said *in their minds.* Don't ever think that, just because you saved her life, you love my sister more than I do."

Facing his oldest friend off with equal coldness, Toby snapped, "How would you feel if I spoke about any other man 'getting' Jazmine?"

Charlie's fists clenched, then released, and he sighed again. "Look, mate, I'm doing the best I can in a hell of a situation. This will be my first decision as King, and the people—and Orakis—will be watching to see what I do. And I'm damned if I'll start a war for your sake, brother or not."

Toby stood in grim silence, waiting for the axe to fall on his life's dream.

"If I changed the law for you and Lia to marry, all the people will see is that under the new rulership nepotism rules. That's what brought down the Orakis dynasty. Papou's disappearance brought on ten years of civil war last century."

There fell the axe. But it wasn't his head that fell bleeding to the ground; it was his heart. Charlie was in a hellhole, and he and Giulia had just deepened it.

Charlie was right. If Toby had been given a choice between eight-million people's lives and the personal happiness of the two people he loved best in the world, he knew the inevitable choice.

He lifted a hand, his gaze on Giulia like an unspoken farewell. "I've put you in a hell of a position and I'm sorry, Rip. It's time I returned to my life back home."

"No, mate. Please. I don't want you to go, and Lia needs you."

He gave a short, bitter laugh. "From everything you've said, I think all she needs is for me to disappear from her life."

"She wasn't eating enough until you came. Surely you've seen she's thinner?"

The words stopped him cold.

* * *

Lia had just heard the same words from her new sister-in-law.

Civil war...

The downfall of the Orakis dynasty...

You can't renounce your position without the permission of the King and House of Hereditary Lords...

Now she knew why Papou had had to disappear completely.

To think of Charlie, her beloved brother, and Jazmine, Max, Theo Angelis, all having to flee from their home.

What hurt most was that, had she kissed Max in front of the wedding guests, in front of the cameras in the middle of the cathedral during the wedding, she wouldn't have been lectured on history and the risks she was taking, or even acting like a princess. All she'd have had in response would have been everyone's amused approval.

But kissing her best friend apparently would all but start a war.

She took a step back, and then another. "Enough, Jazmine, I understand." *Shut down, turn off.* She knew it was wrong, but she couldn't help it. If she didn't disappear emotionally for a while, she'd break.

Jazmine bit her lip. "Lia, you know we—"

She held up a hand for Jazmine to stop. She dragged in a breath, two, trying to control herself. She'd made enough public displays for one night.

But as she turned to the doors, she saw Theo Angelis coming over to her in his wheelchair, his face a mixture of steely determination and loving concern, and knew it must be said. "If you send Toby away, I'll disappear, as Papou did," she said fiercely.

The King wheeled to a stop. Even the royal minder behind him gaped.

The King's eyes snapped with anger. "Don't make empty threats at me, girl."

"Do it and you'll discover just how much my grandfather's child I am." The continued silence assured her she'd made her point. She turned to leave.

"Someone saw him kissing you that first day," the King said, stopping her in her tracks in turn. "One of Orakis's spies, or it could have been one of the Lords' paid eyes and ears. Someone's unhappy. There's been a threat against his life."

Lia froze. She couldn't move, couldn't speak. A shard of ice pierced her soul.

"Given our history, it's no empty threat." The King spoke with compassion, yet was inflexible. "The people demand certain standards from us. You *are* a princess. You must behave as one."

One shiver after another raced through her entire body. Oh, God; God help her.

Tick, tick, tick...

The clock moved backward and she was fifteen again, facing the truth: she could never have the boy she loved with all her heart and soul. *But now, loving him could kill him.*

And her ancient enemy came back to taunt her, as her stomach clenched and she felt bile rising.

"I'll be back to see you off," she whispered to Jazmine, and left the ballroom with slow, deliberate grace, like the princess she must be.

Toby watched her leave, saw the uneven step, and felt sick himself. He knew where Giulia was going...

He had to go to her—but he was being watched. He couldn't follow her, unless he went round by another way, or unless he made the perfect excuse.

As the best man, he had that.

He gathered the eleven groomsmen—the only one he knew at all was Max, the others were noblemen and politicians from around Europe, chosen for political purposes, as Jazmine's bridesmaids had been—and he told them a few certain Australian wedding customs without which Charlie wouldn't feel properly married, and where the "accessories" could be found.

The men all laughed and agreed to help. Even Max smiled

with enthusiasm, as if they were friends, yet he must have seen Giulia kissing Toby on the balcony…

The eleven noblemen and politicians left in groups of three and four at each door, causing a logistical nightmare for their respective minders. Toby watched his security detail going bananas trying to discreetly follow them. Any moment now, all of the groomsmen would have their arms filled with tin cans, ribbons and spray-paint cans with which to decorate the honeymoon helicopter, freaking out every Secret Service agent with the potential for explosive materials.

And so, for the ten seconds his security detail was distracted by the earpieces going berserk, he slipped out to the balcony, hopped it, dropped the twelve feet to the ground—peanuts for him, even in a tux—and came back in via the front.

He'd have about ninety seconds to find her before they found him.

When he found her door locked, he ran to the end of the corridor, hopped to the first balcony and leapt from one balcony to the next until he reached hers. He knew it would be locked, but Giulia could never stand a stuffy room, even in winter. And the weather was still unseasonably warm for autumn.

Hanging by his hands from the corner of the railing, he kicked his legs into the bedroom window, gripped tight, and swung upside down for a moment before doing a sit-up. Hands gripped the sash; he was in.

Outside her private bathroom, he heard the sounds he'd dreaded returning for more than a decade. Muffled, painful retching…

The bathroom door was locked, too. So he kicked it in, grabbed it by the handle in case it went off its hinges and fell on her, and pushed it against the wall before he strode to her. She hung over the toilet bowl, retching up nothing.

Oh, God, no; God, no, please…

"Toby," she croaked, and vomited again.

He gathered her into his arms and sat back down with her

on his lap. "Still more?" he asked simply, knowing this was not the time to berate her or ask questions she couldn't handle.

She started to nod, then leaned into the bowl again.

He wanted to hit someone about now, to scream, "See? She needs me, you morons!" but time was of the essence. They had to be back at the wedding party within half an hour or the situation would escalate, more pressure would be put on her, and the cycle would be worsened. If his short acquaintance with the King was any indication, he'd kick Toby out and order in an army of specialists: people who knew their job, but didn't know Giulia. And she'd just get sicker.

He couldn't tell anyone. This had to remain between them alone.

Charlie would know the moment he saw his sister's face, but he couldn't help that. He'd go on his honeymoon worried sick and share his fears with Jazmine. The two of them would call twice or three times a day to make sure she was eating. All of which would make Giulia feel worse, by showing their worry, love and fear of losing her, their beautiful, special Giulia, so wise about everyone except herself.

It was time for damage minimisation, not damage control.

When the spasm passed, he held her and stroked her hair, which was falling from its perfect chignon. "I'm here, beloved. I'm here."

Her head fell to his shoulder. "For how long?" she whispered.

If he knew her, she knew him too, he thought wryly. "Do you honestly believe I'd ever leave you like this?" *Or at all,* his mind added, accepting a truth he'd barely been able to face when he'd made that vow to the doctor years before: *Will you still give her everything she needs when she's sleeping with another man?*

Even then?

Could you give her what she needs when she's having another man's baby, sharing his bed?

Looking at her now, there was only one answer.

Yes…even then.

"It's not the anorexia." She could never speak above a whisper when she went into shutdown. She was so ashamed of her weakness, her imperfection.

He kissed her forehead, her cheek. "Tell me."

"You know. I know Charlie told you."

He nodded. No wonder she was throwing up. "It's not going to happen." He'd spend his life in prison for killing Orakis before he'd let him within touching distance of her.

"There's only one way to stop it."

Max. He felt like throwing up too. But he pulled himself together. Not for the sake of eight-million people—he wasn't that noble; not even for the best friend he'd ever had—but for the sake of the woman in his arms. The woman he'd loved with hope for half his life, and would love without hope for the rest of it. And right now a double prison sentence seemed a preferable option to night after night alone thinking of what she'd endure with Orakis—or, God help him, enjoy with Max.

The quiver that ran through her wasn't like when they'd been dancing, in the sweet lead-up to exquisite, unforgettable kisses. "I wish they'd never found us. I'm glad Charlie's happy," she rasped, "But why should he get happiness and I get Jazmine's choice?"

Trying to make her smile, he said softly, "Including the rough fireman from Sydney as option three?"

"The only way we could marry now is if we disappear, change our names and our lives—and that's impossible. I'd have to leave Charlie and Jazmine to face all the problems on their own." She sighed. "You wouldn't cope with it if you couldn't keep being a fireman. You'd hate me for it sooner or later. And it's not in me to run away from my responsibilities, Toby, even for you."

No, it wasn't. She'd hate herself for life if she left Charlie to face this mess alone. The only destruction she'd ever wreaked was on herself, never others.

"And that's not all." She leaned over the toilet and dry-retched again once, twice, until she fell back against him, heaving deep breaths. "Someone knows you kissed me, proposed to me the other week. They've threatened your life."

Strange that, though the shock ran through him like a streak of lightning, he wasn't surprised. In a place like Hellenia, where emotions ran as high as expectation, he'd known a commoner courting a princess would have massive repercussions.

But Giulia was throwing up for the first time in ten years, and to him that was a far greater threat than anything a reactionary Hellenican could throw at him. "Let's not think about that now. Let's just concentrate on getting you well again."

Giulia lifted her head and stared at him. "Get me well? I'm not *sick*. I told you, this isn't anorexia, it's shock. Toby, someone's threatening your life. You need to go home right after Charlie and Jazmine's coronation."

And though he knew it wasn't an idle or empty threat, he'd faced death on a near-daily basis for years, in factory fires, house- and bushfires out of control. He'd been to twenty funerals of guys with young families, comforted grieving widows of his mates. Giulia didn't know, couldn't understand that, to a fireman death was an intimate enemy, a hated friend. It happened too often for it to hold terror for him the way it did for her. "I'm not going anywhere while you need me. Don't let it bother you so much, Giulia. I know how to look after myself."

"From a fire, yes—but how do you protect yourself from a bullet or a bomb?" Her mouth tightened. "Don't patronise me, Toby. I don't need you to protect me." She pushed at his chest and got to her feet. "We'll need a carpenter to fix the door."

He was sitting at her feet. Feeling like a supplicant was something he hated. He'd been that when he'd gone to the Costas at fifteen and had asked if he could live with them. He never wanted to be lower than anyone ever again. He rose to his feet and stood behind her, watching her. "What *do* you need from me?" he demanded, to remind her of the kiss half an hour ago. To see how she'd respond.

She turned to the massive, marble double sink, opened the mirrored doors above and got out her toothbrush. As she applied toothpaste, she said, "What I need is what I thought we'd been having the past few years—I want us to be friends who care for each other, not for me to be the one you constantly watch in case I get sick again. And I need you to go home."

"Friends? Then what was the kiss about?" he snarled, ignoring her demand that he go home.

She brushed her teeth and rinsed her mouth. Then she pulled out her make-up from behind the mirrored doors and began making repairs to her face. "I don't really know. Maybe the last blast from a fifteen-year-old girl who wanted nothing more than to kiss the boy she was so crazy about. Maybe the girl needed that before the woman could move on."

The words hit him like a sudden punch to the gut because he didn't know if they were true. Because they could be true. Because he could have had the love of his life—she could have been his wife, the mother of his children already—if only he'd kissed her back on that damned New Year's Eve for longer than a few seconds.

Lia spoke with a cool detachment that belied her pounding heart. Would he believe her? She willed him with every part of her being to believe it. She had to make him want to go home, to feel he didn't belong here. Even if she had to convince him she wanted to marry Max, she'd do it for his sake…and for her own. The thought of living a life without him—somewhere in the world—was unbearable.

Even if he's with another woman?

Yes, she acknowledged to herself, almost without pain—well, compared to the other option. She'd survived seeing him with other women before. She could do it again just so long as he was alive and well.

Then the pain slammed into her heart, crying *No* at the top of its voice. She was going crazy. She had to get out, get away from him. She needed to hold him and never let go, beg him to stay. She couldn't, *couldn't* bear it if he died.

"Charlie and Jazmine should be about to leave. We need to lead the confetti tossing." She couldn't control the quiver in her voice, and didn't expect to. Neither would he. Their love was too strong to let go easily; they both knew that, friends or lovers.

"Giulia, don't do this to us." His voice was rough, hurting. "Not now when we finally have a chance."

Oh, God help me do this…

She closed her eyes. "There is no chance. There never was an 'us,' and never will be."

"Then tell me where my life ends and yours begins." It was a quiet voice, but no less demanding for that; no less absolute truth, pulling her heart from her chest. "Tell me where we divide, because I don't see one part of my life that isn't filled with you."

You won't have a life if they kill you.

"We divided when you dated those other women, Toby—and we end at the place where I'm marrying Max." Before he could speak again she walked out, wrenching open her bedroom door, all but running past the waiting security detail and down the hall and stairs to where the farewell crowd was gathering preparatory to heading to the lawn where the crazily decorated chopper waited.

CHAPTER FIVE

"CAN-NO one control that ridiculous animal?"

The King sounded irritable, and no wonder. Not only was it well after midnight, closer to one before the last guests who weren't staying in the palace had left, but the tea room stank. After hours of confinement in a kennel during the wedding, Puck was ready for action the moment Lia released him.

He'd not exactly been the comforter she'd sought when she'd run to the kennel.

She called him, but though she'd walked him and let him relieve himself after letting him out, to Puck release meant at least half an hour of frolic and nervous leg-liftings in every conceivable corner and on every furniture leg before he settled.

Obviously still in a black mood, Toby called him, hard and commanding. Puck came, but bolted as soon as he saw the leash in Toby's hand. Max tried, but he was smothering laughter, and Puck treated his half-hearted attempts with the contempt they deserved.

"Puck."

The deep, hard voice was used to instant obedience, and even Puck slithered to a confused halt. His head tilted; the bright, intelligent eyes sought out the voice.

"Come."

The dog tilted his head further, testing limits. Awaiting the second and third call before he'd consider it.

The King never repeated himself. She supposed he'd never had to, in his long life of duty and privilege. He merely held the dog's eye and waited.

Puck blinked—he really did—and slowly, showing his protest, he crossed the room to the King, and waited in front of the wing-backed chair.

"Sit." It wasn't harsh, just a simple, confident command.

After a few moments, Puck sat.

"Stay."

Having no idea what it meant—he only stayed anywhere when he was asleep—the dog tilted his head again, considering.

The King held his hand in front of the dog's face, but didn't repeat the word. Not even for a dog would he lower his dignity.

Evidently Puck got the message. He remained sitting in front of the uplifted hand, waiting for the next piece of attention, for praise.

"Good boy," was all the King said, but Puck licked the hand in front of him: an adoring transfer of drool.

Despite the trauma of the day, or maybe because of it, Lia started laughing. "Could you train him for me, please? He's never obeyed anyone before."

The old man looked at her from behind his glasses. "He knows you don't mean what you say. You tell him something and then let him have his way. The dog has to understand that you know what's best for him, even when he doesn't know why. He needs you to be in control, to give him direction."

Lia felt her colour rise. They both knew he wasn't talking about the dog.

"It doesn't matter if they're purebreds or the scruffiest of mongrels." He flicked a glance at Toby, who didn't move or respond in any way. "They need to know who's master. They want the safety of boundaries, of rules that don't bend or change."

"Interesting theory," she said, short and terse.

The King looked down to where Puck sat staring at him in canine devotion.

She put her Royal Albert cup of hot chocolate back in its saucer untasted. "It seems he's chosen his master, Your Majesty. Keep him."

The King didn't answer, but she felt the hurt in his silence.

Could they all see how she could barely stand to look at the King, couldn't bring herself to use the intimate family name of Theo Angelis? She'd felt the resentment since he'd told her about the death threats. It might not be his fault, but it *felt* like it was: the universe arranging itself on the side of what the King wanted for her.

Now he'd even taken her dog from her.

"We need to discuss when your wedding will take place." The King stared hard, first at Max then Lia.

Walking out of the room would make her look childish, and would put her in a weak position. She'd had enough of that tonight. "This isn't the right time."

"There won't be a better time. The sooner you put your teenage crush behind you and become a woman, the princess you are, the better."

"Marrying a near-stranger could never be seen as a reasoned act for a woman or a princess," she replied with a quiet dignity she'd noticed he found hard to argue with. "If by becoming a woman you mean doing what you want of me, just say so. Then we can discuss who's behaving like the child in this scenario."

Dead silence met her challenge.

"I agree with Lia."

Max's words startled her into looking round. Max met the King's challenging gaze with cool, well-bred wisdom. "It was obvious to everyone tonight that Lia isn't ready to marry me. It would make us look ridiculous to force the issue now."

Hot colour now scorched her cheeks. "Max…"

"There's no need to apologise." He smiled at her, with no shadows. "Charlie stepped up to the plate because he loves Jazmine as well as the country. You've done a magnificent job with all the duties thrown your way, but your heart isn't in a royal marriage of convenience." He turned back to the King. "This is the twenty-first century. The era of arranged marriages, with kings' mistresses and queens' discreet lovers, went out a hundred years ago. It only ends in messy, public divorce."

The King's cheeks whitened, and Lia frowned at the seeming overreaction. Then he snapped, "It might have gone out of fashion in most of Western Europe, but so did most of the monarchies around the same time. Is that what we want here?"

Max sighed. "I didn't say that, Theo Angelis. I only said I won't force Lia into a marriage she isn't ready for." He smiled at her, and despite the long, hard day it had been, filled with such joy and despair, she smiled back.

Toby stood abruptly. "Goodnight, everyone."

As he left the room, Lia ached with the need to explain again, to give him the uncomplicated goodnight cuddles they'd once shared, but she couldn't. They couldn't go back, and she couldn't make herself try to heal the breach.

She saw the King's small smile. He didn't bother to hide his satisfaction at Toby's desertion, and her silence.

The gym was quiet, dark apart from the light of a full moon, flooding through the high, west-facing windows as it began to slowly sink, heading towards dawn.

Clad in warm-up clothes and stockinged feet, carrying the portable CD player she'd found in her room the day she'd arrived, Lia closed the door on her minders.

Within a minute she had all she needed: a big, empty space

filled with only the silvery spotlight provided by nature. She pulled on her points, tipped her head back and lifted her hair into a band. A press of the remote control, and the room filled with soft classical music.

It was so long, so long since she'd been herself, since she'd had an hour without pressure or expectation.

She lifted her arms to the moon and lifted up on her toes, pas seul to arabesque, and with a movement she became part of the night.

Every part of Toby ached, just watching her. She was a wood nymph dancing between the moonlight and the stars. A fairy princess weaving the magic of her own unique, living beauty. So close, always so close, yet just out of reach.

Sleep had eluded him, so he'd come here to work off too many weeks of stress. He hadn't turned on the lights. The darkness suited his mood; his heart was filled with loss and anger and a love that owned every pore and cell of him.

And then, like a silent miracle, she'd walked into the darkened gym. Once again she'd come to him when his heart was screaming for her.

She'd always had that gift. Somehow she always knew when to come to him and give him hope when he needed it most.

She'd been all of twelve when she'd found him at the local park in Ryde, punching out a classmate, Mick Reilly, for making fun of his tears. How she'd known he desperately needed someone—needed her—he hadn't known, then or now. But some dim part of him had known that, somehow, she'd come.

"Toby," she'd said softly, when he'd been on the verge of losing control, so lost in black grief he hadn't known what he was doing. The gentle, husky voice had stopped his fist mid-punch. She'd had that knack with him from the first day they'd met. He couldn't upset little Lia with the dark violence in his soul.

And "little Lia" had taken him away from Mick, away from curious eyes, and had made him tell her what was wrong. When she'd heard about his parents' divorce, and their demands that he choose a parent over the other, she'd seen the solution without trying. "Come and live with us, Toby. You can share Charlie's room until Dad and Papou build you one."

He remembered trying to laugh. At fifteen, full of hormones, anger and loss, it had seemed so simple an answer. Only a kid would have found it; it was such a miracle only a kid would believe it could happen. "Why would your dad and grandfather build anything for me? They won't want me. I hang around your place too much as it is."

"We like having you. You're family, Toby. Come home now and see." And she'd smiled at him, had taken his hand, led him home, and pulled off the first miracle he'd ever known with her unswerving faith.

That day was the first time Giulia had made him lose his breath with her wisdom, her smile and her touch, but far from the last.

Looking back now, he wondered if he'd fallen in love that day, because when he'd seen her unconscious in hospital and had known this love was for life, it had felt so right, so inevitable; he hadn't been able to believe he hadn't seen it before.

Fifteen years of small miracles; the one certainty in his life had been that Giulia always knew when to come to him. Half a lifetime of looking at her, wondering what she saw in him to need; but she did, and every day she turned to him had felt like a gift from God—because, no matter how much she needed him, he needed her more.

Like tonight. He'd ached and burned so badly, and she'd danced into his waking nightmare and made it beautiful.

This wasn't the princess, not the woman of duty and honour and sacrifice who'd told him to go home. In her ballet gear, her hair scraped back, this was his shy, giving, wonderful Giulia, the girl who danced into his heart whenever she moved.

He watched and ached as she spun and leaped across the moonlit space. His whole body twitched with the need to go to her, but he couldn't bear to break her spell with clumsy words or movement.

She danced on, oblivious grace, a shadow of spun glass, eternal memory.

He'd never seen anything more beautiful than this woman moving amid the moonlight and stars. This moment was so perfect as she soared above the night sky for an audience of one, the man who loved every single part of her and might never again come closer to her than this, a distant watcher.

Yet he'd wait the rest of his life for a single chance.

And then he saw what she was dancing: the first act of *Giselle,* the innocent girl with her lover, the man she didn't know was far out of her reach, the man who'd send her mad with love unrequited, unfulfilled.

But she danced it alone, a lonely Giselle…

Was he awake or dreaming? His hands took her waist; there was no gasp to break the dream. Natural as breathing, she leaped high and he lifted her above him as he'd practised with her so many times when she'd won the part but there hadn't been a male dancer tall enough to lift her. He'd joined the troupe for a season: an awkward Loys to exquisite Giselle, the man high above her yet unworthy of her love.

To the beat of the music, he brought her down against his body, clinging for a moment before she broke away, elusive, a graceful shadow, woman-child, peasant princess. Then her hand stretched back to him and he caught her, spinning her to him, and she leaped away after one perfect moment.

The ache of inevitability filled him, his chest and throat, as he tried to be worthy of being her partner, to have her in his arms one last time.

This was their story in reverse.

Yet when she pirouetted around him, her long-fingered hands touched the sweaty old T-shirt covering his skin, as slow and longing as if the differences did not exist or matter. She came face to face with him and opened her eyes.

Was it Giselle or his Giulia, with all that sweet yearning, offering her lips to him? He brought her to him with shaking hands and kissed her as Loys would have, swift, fleeting, aching for more. But she fluttered away, a girl in the bloom of life and love, believing there would be tomorrow, there would always be tomorrow.

There would be no more kisses. Tomorrow she would discover the deceit: Loys would become Albrecht and she'd die of madness. She'd save his life and then go for ever from his reach. Tomorrow Giulia would become a princess, and he…

Oh, God, it was their story.

Yet still he stumbled through the motions, awaiting each chance to touch her as she danced amid the stars.

As they wove harmoniously together in the slow-waning moonlight, another person unable to sleep watched them through the modern miracle of camera.

After dismissing the amused night guard, Max stood riveted. Such luminous perfection between woman and man; the spotlight of God was on them as they danced. Somehow in the shadows of the past he saw the girl and boy they'd been dancing beside them. It would always be this way for them, no matter what a king willed, no matter what honour or duty demanded.

No matter whom she married.

The Grand Duke, currently fourth in line to the throne but who knew himself to be the King's puppet, watched the second—no, the third—woman who would have been his wife dance away with her heart intact, and wondered what was missing in him.

Whatever it was, he would not be the one to destroy their final hour together.

Max switched off the cameras as the music faded. He didn't want to see the magic vanish and duty return to the eyes of a woman who would never want him. This night, this hour, belonged to Lia and Toby. This was their story alone.

"Thank you, Toby."

Her voice was rich and sweet, and quivered in a husky but definite farewell.

He'd known it would happen. With the return of the woman had come the principles he wouldn't change if he could; they made her the wonderful person she was. But his lovely Giselle was gone, and he was left feeling like a fool.

Barely able to stand it, knowing the princess and woman were intertwined so tightly he couldn't even see between them, he nodded. He wouldn't look at her.

"Toby, please."

"Don't. It's not your fault. It's no one's fault," he said wearily. "I'll be leaving for home as soon as Charlie's coronation is over."

"Maybe it was meant to be this way. All these years, and we have only a day."

"A day?" he shot back bitterly. "Not even an hour and it was over."

"It's always the wrong time for us," she whispered.

He laughed without humour. "You're right. So many times I've tried to tell you, and life changed. Most recently on the night out in Sydney we never had, the ten-year celebration of your release from the clinic. I'd planned the whole night around telling you how I feel. But you were gone."

After a few moments, she spoke, her voice filled with sadness. "So many times I tried to tell you too, and something came between us."

He still couldn't look at her; he could barely stand the pain of being near her, not touching her. "You mean the women I dated? You said they divided us."

"It doesn't matter now."

"It does." He swung around, taking her by the shoulders, aching and hurting just at the sight of her sad beauty in the shaft of pale, dying moonlight, with the warm, silky feel of her skin in his hands. "Now is all we have, Giulia."

She sighed, turning her face slightly so she didn't look at him. "So ridiculous, isn't it? After fifteen years where we could have spoken, we choose now, when it can't make any difference."

"It makes a difference to me."

Slowly she shook her head. "You don't know what you're asking. I've kept it locked inside for so long…"

He cupped her averted face in his hands. "Tomorrow could be too late. Tell me, Giulia. Please."

Her face was ethereal in the waning moonlight. A ghost of Giselle, about to fade before his eyes as she sighed, and finally spoke the words he'd waited almost eleven years to hear.

"I was so far and so deep in love with you I couldn't see any other man, could never bear the thought of touching anyone else," she said quietly. "I wanted to tell you so many times, but I'd almost destroyed our friendship once by kissing you."

"*Was* in love with me?" His voice was rough with all the might-have-beens.

"Was." She sighed. "Until Mandy." She turned to him with a brave smile. "But she didn't last. We did. I'm still here, we're friends."

Mandy was the first girl he'd dated since Giulia's release from the clinic, three years after she'd come home. "I have to know. Did I hurt you?"

Her mouth quirked in a travesty of the smile she'd given him moments before. "I wanted to die for a few days." She bit her lip, shook her head. "Stupid girl, huh? It's a shame I didn't make the ballet. It would have fulfilled my desire for drama." She looked up when he didn't respond: she knew. "I didn't die, Toby. I grew up. Dating Mandy was probably the best gift you could have given me at the time."

He drew her close. "I'm so sorry, so damned sorry, Giulia. I was the stupid one. I thought you didn't want me. I thought you'd turn from me, say you were sorry and I'd lose you. I thought—" He felt sick, but knew if it wasn't said now it never would be. "I couldn't risk stressing you to the point where you'd stop eating again."

She frowned and looked fully at him for the first time since they'd danced, and his heart jerked at the sad question hovering inside her. "Can't you ever see beyond the anorexia to see *me?* Couldn't you tell me, and trust that I'd deal with it as an adult?"

She sounded more sorrowful than incensed, so he took the chance. "I should have, but I couldn't." He kissed her hair as he murmured, "Dr Evans said I had to wait for you to speak. He said if you didn't want me, the threat of losing my friendship could make you sick again. He said the fear of losing me could kill you."

And she'd proved that tonight, getting sick for the first time in years at hearing about the death threats. She could deny the anorexia, claim it was shock, and probably she was right in part. But she hadn't eaten since; he'd watched her during supper, watched her playing with the hot chocolate, not even touching the cakes or fruit.

Giulia stilled in his arms. For a few moments he couldn't even feel her breathe. When she spoke, the words weren't filled with the anger he half-expected. "Before today, I'd have yelled at you for believing him, when you threw out all the other rules with me and got it right. I'd have been angry that you took the word of someone who didn't know me." She lifted her face to press her cheek against his. "But today I know how that fear takes over everything."

He nodded, moving his cheek, drinking in her skin. "I'd rather have the hell on earth of knowing you're halfway across the world and I can't see or touch you than know you're gone."

"That's how I feel," she whispered. "Even if you have someone else…and we both know it will happen."

"No, damn it, *no*." He pulled back to look into her eyes, feeling the betrayal of his love without it ever being spoken. "You can't believe that."

She smiled sadly and shrugged, a weary, hopeless gesture. "I don't pretend to be unforgettable, much as I'd like to be— and you aren't the kind of man to be alone for long. Women adore you, they always have, and you love them too. Especially those bubbly blondes you go for."

"I don't go for blondes, Giulia, bubbly or otherwise. I haven't seen anyone but you for years. I only dated those women because they were nothing like you!" Then seeing how she'd taken his words, he blurted, "No, Giulia, I meant I chose them because, though I'd lost hope with you, I couldn't stand the reminders of you. No woman could ever replace you for me." *Because I was, and still am, so far and so deep in love with you I barely noticed what they looked like—and they all knew it.*

"You lost hope with me without ever telling me?" she whispered. "Did I turn you off so badly somehow?"

"No, beloved, you don't understand!" But how could he explain what he didn't understand himself? Why *had* he lost hope?

Because I was so damn scared of losing you, I couldn't speak.

I didn't want them, Giulia. Can't you see? I only want you. I love only you.

The look on her face, saying what she must for his sake, lost in the fear of killing him, withered the words on his tongue. He'd been there, done that, missed her every signal of pain when he'd dated the women he could barely remember. But Giulia remembered those girls, and she wouldn't hear his words of love now if he shouted them at her.

"There's nothing shameful about preferring blondes, Toby, or girls who don't want to stay at home or go on bushwalks. I dealt with that reality years ago. You don't find me physically attractive, or you didn't until recently. But you've always liked outgoing blondes. One day you'll marry one of them and have children." She kissed his cheek. "And then you can visit, our kids will be friends like we are."

Speechless, he watched her pack up her kit and leave the gym. The moon dipped behind the trees, and he was left in darkness, wondering if he'd ever get it right with her. He had to make her look beyond her damaged self-vision to the brave, beautiful, wise and giving woman she was, to make her see how lovable and worthy of love she was.

He was running out of time. There seemed no hope of his dream coming true. But if he could give her that gift before the King kicked him out, then if she had to go into marriage with a stranger—God help him—she'd have the strength to meet that man as an equal. And when he was gone, she wouldn't waste away to nothing.

He stood in the darkness, wondering how he'd had a best friend and almost-lover beside him so many years and it was only now he was starting to see the real woman inside that quiet heart.

CHAPTER SIX

GIULIA was magnificent—but something was wrong.

During the past two weeks, Toby had organised his work-tour schedule to coincide with as many of Giulia's visits to towns and villages as possible. Today was another such time, and he'd had a bad feeling for hours.

Though she was saying and doing everything right, though the people and press adored her as much today as yesterday, his bad feeling grew until he was barely functioning. So he'd handed the reins to one of the retired senior-firefighters from the nearby town. Followed by his minders—Giulia and Charlie had insisted on his having protection—he strode to the Town Hall where the logistics of keeping the third and fourth in line to the throne wasn't such a nightmare.

She stood in the centre of an admiring circle, mostly consisting of women and children, smiling and giving from the heart. They all adored her, and the press lapped it up. She was so much like another beloved princess, shy and awkward but so eager to help, with a heart so true and loving the people responded in kind.

Yet he could see the stress taking its toll on her. The women were kissing her hands, thanking her with tears for being a princess who cared so much for her people. She'd taken on the House of Hereditary Lords. Giulia had fought long and hard with the King and the Lords to make the change to a four-hundred-year-old law that allowed male relatives to sell off a woman's land, house or possessions and keep the proceeds.

Now, thanks to Giulia, no man could act as a woman's financial representative without the woman's signed affidavit, witnessed by an independent lawyer to prevent duress.

But today's visit had been a tough one. She'd visited the graves of those who'd been killed in the civil war—a reminder that she was helping bring peace to the nation. But her life could never be her own again. Although she was saying and doing everything right, her foot was tapping; her hands were discreetly wiping on her skirt.

She only perspired to the hands when something overwhelmed her. What was worrying her so much? He strode over, but her minders stopped him before he could get close. One put a note into his hand. It was terse, to the point:

Being seen with me could kill you, or hurt these women and children. Please stop following me!

She was already on edge, and no wonder. They were in Orakis territory. Since she'd met with Orakis last week, sweetly asking his permission to set up the refuge, all of them could see Orakis wasn't smitten with Giulia's title alone. He couldn't keep his eyes from her, even when talking to the King.

He'd have to go through the acceptable option.

The crowd around Max parted for him; they all knew Toby was their future King's closest friend. He spoke low, so only Max would hear it. "Giulia has a headache. They only come when she's upset about something. Go to her."

Max flicked a glance at Giulia. "She looks fine to me. The crowd can be a bit much sometimes."

He stared at Max, wondering if the man was blind. "Trust

me. She has a stress headache. She needs to go back and rest or it will turn to a migraine."

Max said with clear impatience now, "She can't go back until we're done here. This is her duty, despite how she feels. Lia has to do her share."

Toby felt his fists clench. "You keep telling yourself that. It suits my purpose. Push her too hard for much longer, and she'll be ready to disappear with me."

"Always so noble, rescuing the trapped princess," Max mocked. "I have better things to do than pander to your fears. Go on, play the hero again—but I doubt she'll appreciate your interference. She's stronger than you know."

"I know her better than you ever will," he said coldly. "I'd go to her, but the King convinced her that being seen with me is dangerous to my health."

Max clicked his tongue. "If you love her so much, why don't you start treating her as a woman? You might be surprised by her reaction."

"You don't have a clue what Giulia needs," Toby snarled. "For God's sake, Max, just ask if she's all right."

He stalked off, unable to stomach the sight of Max bonding with her.

Late that night, Lia stood outside the secret door, hoping that after more than an hour of opening to empty rooms and wrong wings she was there at last.

Jazmine had showed her the secret passageways while they'd been still getting to know each other. If her sister-in-law knew why she was here now, she'd wish those nights of laughter and girlish fun had never happened.

She couldn't stand the days and nights—especially the nights. All her life, she'd been surrounded by family love, but since she'd come here she'd felt smothered and starved, given everything she didn't want and nothing she *did* want.

She fulfilled all her duties. She was eating, as she assured

Charlie in his anxious calls. She wouldn't ruin her brother's honeymoon by collapsing when he needed her to take up the slack.

But she wasn't sleeping more than three hours a night. Her body didn't fill her clothes. She'd dropped a size. According to her specialist, whom she'd called today, her weight was bordering on dangerously low.

"You're stressed, Lia...Your Highness," Dr Evans had added respectfully. "I've been following your progress and your pictures say it all. If you don't find a way to unwind, you'll be back in hospital within days. Toby's there, isn't he? Talk to him, Lia. Do something fun, as the two of you always did before."

His bluntness had shocked her, woke her from a walking nightmare. She was doing everything right, eating to reassure everyone that she wasn't anorexic again, but she spent every night pacing the floor, dancing with a frantic emptiness or fighting tears. Aching to be with the one person she couldn't, because it could start a war again or get him killed. Just seeing him near her during her public visits triggered stress headaches that no amount of medication would control.

She pulled at the old stone handle. It opened with a slight, protesting creak.

"What the hell—?" Smothered words, but the deep growl she needed to hear.

She drew in a breath. "It's me. Close the curtains." When she heard the scraping sound end, she came into the room.

He'd just come back from a night run, by the looks of it, his sweatshirt and tracksuit damp with perspiration. He looked intensely masculine. Hot and edible.

And yet through the physical yearning she felt a pang, wishing he could have knocked on her door like the old days and asked if she wanted to run.

At this moment, just a walk would fill her soul. Viewing

mountains and forests from behind the dark glass of bullet-proof cars made her ache with loss.

"There are secret passages in the palace?" His voice was light, as if he expected her to tell him off—or maybe it was in deference to the minders outside. "You've got to be kidding me. This entire country is a conspiracy theorist's playground."

She covered her mouth to stifle the laugh and walked to him. "I knew you'd appreciate it. Charlie's only been in once, would you believe?"

Toby shook his head. "That man needs imagination."

"Want to come and see?" she asked softly.

His eyes held hers, deep as an Outback sky, and as intense. "Only if you're asking me what I think you are. Because if I'm alone in a dark passage with you for longer than a minute I'm going to kiss you again."

She felt heat filling her body, her breath disappear. She ached and burned and longed. He was the only man she'd ever fantasised about as her lover, the groom at the end of the aisle in all her wedding dreams. She opened her mouth to say yes...

"Please," she said as her conscience kicked in, the memories of every reason why she couldn't say yes. "Can we please just go for a walk and talk? There's a path that leads to the forest. Jazmine doesn't think anyone but the four of us knows about it." She took a step to him, her face lifted to his, her hand reaching for him. "I haven't even been on a walk in months. I don't feel like *me* anymore."

The old Toby would have responded by taking her hand and giving her his wonderful, heart-singing smile. This Toby kept looking at her, his eyes shadowed.

Unable to stand any more scrutiny after weeks and months of it by everyone she knew and millions she didn't, she turned away. "Don't worry, it was a stupid idea." She laughed with a bitterness she couldn't control. "Fifty-million euros and a tiara is obviously all a girl needs for happiness. Goodnight."

She headed back to the passage.

"Giulia."

She closed her eyes, couldn't turn back. "What?" she asked huskily.

Nothing in her entire life felt as beautiful as his hand taking hers and lifting it to his mouth. "Just so we're clear, I still want to kiss you—but I'll wait until you want it too." And he smiled at her.

Wanted him to kiss her? She almost laughed again. Some days it seemed it was all she could think about. When she was surrounded by strangers expecting gracious words, or to take some personal part of her home with them, thinking of Toby kept her sane. She dreamed of kissing him, touching him, disappearing with him—leaving this life she could barely handle, hiding out in their house in Sydney and making love all night without cameras or minders or kings telling them they couldn't.

But right now she'd take what she could have with him. If it was friendship, she'd make it enough.

She opened the door to the passage again. "You have to be very quiet," she added as he came into the cave-like maw and filled it with his presence, his strength. "If they hear us…"

"Secret assignations with my Giulia. I'd love it if it weren't so ironic," he said, dipping his voice so it was low, intimate.

Lia swallowed the aching. He was so close the current of warm wanting arced between them like a fickle summer-wind.

Without a word, she led him down the stairs to the passage itself, keeping his hand in hers.

"How do you know where you're going? It seems as if it's a complete labyrinth of passages leading nowhere."

She felt the soft rumble of his voice like a long, warm shiver through her, resting low in her belly, hot and heavy. "Jazmine had only one rule: if you're going out to the forest, follow the fresh air and smell of pine."

"Ah."

The single word intensified the ache...fifteen years of aching that had led to only two kisses, threats against his life and the grim spectre of war reignited.

She kept her face turned from him as she found the way through scent alone to the outside passage. She was glad he couldn't see the shimmer of loss in her eyes, the useless longing to have their time, that kiss eleven years ago, over again. If she'd had her dreams, maybe she'd have got past this—this endless fascination that they could be more than the most beautiful and dearest of friends.

But oh, that kiss...

They came out into the cave that was the doorway to the forest on the palace's northern boundary. Made awkward and stupid by longings she couldn't control, she pushed aside the heavy, hanging vines that covered a space just large enough for them to slip through. "This way."

They walked in silence down a thin path through a forest of pine, spruce and fir, each trunk a new and beautiful shade beneath the shadows and moonlight, the branches and leaves above shimmering with starlight and the beams coming down between the thin, scudding clouds.

Filled with the deep quiet around them, they walked for almost an hour until Lia felt her senses fill with the serenity she'd missed for so long.

At the end of the path, they found a small dell, so tiny they'd have passed it by day, but by night it was a scene from a magical kingdom.

"Oh." Her gaze drank in the vision: moonbeams and shadows over a thick circle of trees crowding around the clearing as if they were listening to a delicious secret. Glistening moss covered the rocks strewn about like fairy seats in the small dell, floodlit in silver. A hint of winter had come; a delicate cobweb of lacy ice lay on the leaves drooping from the lower branches, half-fallen like tiny stalactites. One gossamer stalactite had fallen, landing in the crevice of a rock, lying sprawled in the little abyss like Tinkerbell waiting in silence for Peter.

The smell of loam and crushed pine-needles filled her spirit, lifting it high.

"Oh, Toby," she breathed, holding tight to his hand, filled with wonder and a sense of oneness, of completion she hadn't known since their last bushwalk in the Blue Mountains nearly five months before.

Slowly, he drew her into the curve of his arm. Lost in the sweet awe, she wrapped her arm around his waist and they held each other, as they always did when they found a marvel on one of their walks. "No one else will ever have this moment or share this perfection. Tomorrow it will be gone, except in our memories. This moment is ours alone."

She smiled up at him. "I love the way you talk to me. It's so beautiful."

He dropped a kiss on her nose. "I learned it from those historical books you love. Remember I read them to you when you were sick? You said you wished a man would speak to you as those heroes did. So I practised until it came naturally to me."

Startled, she realised he'd spoken the truth. He'd never talked this way until she'd left the clinic.

Terrified to believe, wanting to doubt him because it kept her safe—kept *him* safe—she asked bluntly, "You've never talked to any of your girlfriends like this?"

His face stilled. "I haven't had a girlfriend since I was nineteen, Giulia. Not since the day you fainted and I knew it was you or no one for me." He laid a finger on her mouth when she started to speak. "I dated a few women, yes. Stupid, selfish and completely a man thing, but if you'd once shown me you wanted me in the past ten years none of those women would be holding a place in your mind. They certainly haven't in mine."

She wheeled away. "You made love to them. You'd stay out until dawn, and then come home and act as if you'd been home all night."

One heartbeat, two; he drew in an audible breath. "With your high principles, I can't expect you to understand, but I only passed time with them. I made it clear to them I was only playing around. I never made *love* to them the way I wanted to make love with you. The way I still want to with you. Only you."

She closed her eyes, fighting temptation. "Do you know how it felt for me, lying there all night waiting for you to come home, my head filled with visions of what you were doing with them?"

He tried to pull her to him, but she stood so stiff in his arms, he let go. "There hasn't been a woman in three years, Giulia. It was too empty," he said huskily behind her ear. "One night I knew I'd rather be cooking and cleaning with you than touching any of them. Why do you think I never dated anyone seriously? It was you, always you. With just one word from you, I'd have been yours for life."

"How was I supposed to believe that when girls as pretty and fun as they were couldn't hold you?" She shuddered, reliving the memory. "No man ever wanted me, and you were with beautiful girls who threw themselves at you all the time. How could I believe you wanted me when you were *intimate* with them?"

He went so still, she felt his heart beating behind her. "Oh, dear God, I did that to you? I made you feel ugly and unwanted?"

Her head fell. She couldn't say it, couldn't bring herself to hurt him.

He snatched her into his arms, kissing her face, her lips, even when she didn't respond. "Oh, my darling, beautiful girl, my love, my Giulia, what the hell have I done to you?"

Unable to bear the exquisite, bittersweet touch, she turned

her face again. "It's not your fault. You tried your best to make me believe I was beautiful."

"But I never showed you I wanted you. So, when you knew I was with other women, it negated everything I told you, made everything empty—turned my words into nonsense, as you called it."

She couldn't bear to look at him. She looked at her fairyland, and wondered why it looked so dark now, so lost. "Yes."

"It's why you don't believe me now when I say how much I want you."

Her nails were digging into her palms with the physical effort to not hold him, comfort him and tell him it was all right, because it never would be again. "Yes."

"I'm sorry, beloved, so stupidly and wretchedly sorry." Toby buried his face in her hair. "I devoted my life to making you feel beautiful and loved, and destroyed it without even knowing. If I'd told you how I felt, if I'd never looked at another woman, you'd be my wife now."

"Probably." She sighed. "Maybe it wouldn't have worked for us anyway." Unable to stand being so close, she gently broke away from him. "We should go back. Thank you for coming with me tonight."

Neither of them spoke as they left their little Neverland behind, turning their faces back to reality.

The numbness left Lia within minutes as her heart became swamped by the sad irony that he'd always been hers, but could and would never *be* hers. With all her heart, she wished Dr Evans had never spoken to Toby—but he had, and ten years of silence on both their parts had led to nothing.

How many signs had she missed through the years? He'd learned to dance for her; how many brothers did that? *Did Charlie?*

He'd read her novels, and adopted the formal speech of the heroes she adored.

He'd learned to cook, but he'd rarely done it alone, unless she was exhausted. He might come home first, but he'd get out the ingredients and wait for her so they could do it together.

A universal truth she'd heard in a movie came back to haunt her: *men and women can't be friends*. All these years she'd wanted him, he'd wanted her too.

I never made love to them the way I wanted to make love with you. Only you.

Believing in a fairy-tale ending for them risked not only his life, but the lives of innocent people—her people—and still she couldn't stop herself dreaming.

"You're thinking about it too," he murmured as she led him back to the cave, the doorway to the passages. "Every time you think of how it could be for us, your breath hitches."

She slipped in past the vines and half-sheltering rock to the cave. "Don't," she murmured, even her voice shaking with need. "I—I need my friend now."

"You'll always have me," he said quietly. "Whatever you want from me is yours for ever. Whether we become lovers, whether you marry me or not, I am always your friend. You never need to question that. I'll always come to you when you need me. For the rest of my life I'll be what you need… friend or lover."

Lover. Ah, that magnificent word, but it was magnificent only when he said it. It was unbearably filled with wonder when it came from the one man she wanted in her life and bed; it offered her the one thing here she did want, because *he* was here.

Nobody would ever know…

"Toby." The name was pure craving. *"Toby…"*

She'd never know if he'd brought her to face him or she'd gone willingly; all she knew was she was in his arms and his mouth was on hers, deep and hot, clinging and tender.

She moaned and wrapped her arms hard around his neck so their bodies twined together as if they were one person. When his tongue touched hers and they joined, she didn't know if he groaned or she did; she didn't know if the pain they'd just been through hurt or heightened it. All she knew was this right, splendid, perfect passion.

It was going to happen. Neither of them could stop it; neither wanted to. And her heart sang at the knowledge: *Toby will be my lover.* It made everything—no, it *was* everything. And at last she knew the bliss she'd read about in her beloved novels; she understood why her grandfather had given up his position for the woman he—

She gasped, her head falling back as his lips trailed over the sensitive skin of her throat, slow, hot kisses over her collarbone, the tender valley between her breasts. *"Ah, Toby!"* she cried, moving against his aroused body with a joy so complete she didn't know where she ended and he began. "Touch me, please touch me."

A sound ripped from her throat when his thumb brushed her hardened nipples. She grabbed his hand, filled it with her swollen breast. "Ah," she moaned, writhing as he moved her pullover aside to nibble her shoulder, his hand caressing her breast.

"Breathe, Giulia," he growled softly, a smile in his voice. "You haven't taken in air properly in over a minute."

She gasped in a breath and smiled at him, brilliant with happiness. "Thank you."

He smiled back, his eyes tender. "Just remember to breathe when we make love, my beloved girl."

"We're going to make love," she whispered, caught in a bliss so poignant she wanted to cry. This kiss, his touch, felt like all her dreams and wishes come to life, all in one hour.

"Yes, we are." She felt the smile on his lips as he kissed her. "Just as soon as you can tell me one thing."

She stilled. This wasn't part of her dreams. A sense of dread filled her. She knew what he'd say, given what she'd told him tonight. "What?"

He looked down at her, the expression a strange mix of soul-deep passion and unmovable resolution. "We'll make love when you can tell me you truly believe that you, Giulia Maria Helena Costa Marandis, are the most beautiful woman in the world to me, and that I desire you more than any woman I've ever known."

CHAPTER SEVEN

"COME here, boy."

Toby stifled the urge to laugh. Even King Angelis had never spoken to him with such condescending force—then he realised the King was calling Puck. Despite the servants who walked the dog and fed him daily, despite Giulia's daily visits, Puck had given his whole heart to the old man who held both their futures in his hands.

Puck slid to a stop from his headlong rush to jump on Toby, turned and rushed back to the King, sitting at his feet. King Angelis smiled and patted the dog's head.

Toby grinned. He'd been an advocate of Pets as Therapy since he'd seen too many old folk burning down their homes when they became vague. A dog to bark its warning was a life-saving measure—but as far as this protected old monarch was concerned, Puck was perfect. There had never been a dog that needed ordering around more, and with King Angelis coming to terms with losing power, having any creature need his guidance was good for the soul.

"Come in and close the door. We have things to discuss, and I don't care for outsiders listening in." When Toby closed the door he barked, "Sit, boy. You're built like a tree. I don't want a crick in my neck every time I see you."

The King wasn't used to looking up to anyone. Keeping a

straight face, Toby sat. This wasn't the time to antagonise the old monarch, not when he'd finally made up his mind to break a fourteen-year-old trust...

Papou and Yiayia would understand. They always knew how I loved Giulia.

The King, oblivious to Toby's inner turmoil, got straight to the point. "Princess Giulia's maid informed security that she wasn't in her room this morning. She's using the secret passages to come to you."

Toby went cold inside. Damn. Giulia had come to him in the night, after a horrendous day. After she'd rejected Orakis's latest attempt to woo her, one of her refuges had mysteriously been blown up; four women had been killed. She'd come to him before dawn, white and shaking: *Hold me, Toby; just hold me.*

"She had a bad day," Toby conceded quietly. "She needed comfort."

"She needs to become stronger if she's going to live here. She's not a child, and she can't go running to you when you're gone."

"As unpalatable as it is to you, sire, I'm not going anywhere as long as Giulia needs me," Toby said bluntly. "She's crushed beneath the workload of royal life and living in the public eye. She'll end up back in hospital if you push her any further."

"If you're referring to her childhood bout of anorexia, it's no such thing now. It's natural for her to be a bit run down with her workload and new life."

"That's a common misconception." Toby handed the King a card from his wallet. "I suggest you have an aide call her specialist. Anorexia nervosa doesn't end. Vomiting and not eating are stress reactions very few anorexics overcome. She's lost five kilos since she came here, and at her height that's in the danger zone." He held the old man's eye, setting the scene for his secret. "Dr Evans will tell you I'm the one she needs most at these times. I won't be the one to break her faith. Will you?"

The King's jaw jutted. "You tap dance around this well, boy. But the truth is you can't stay away from her."

He didn't bat an eyelash. "I've made no secret of my feelings for her." He waited for the rest. The old man obviously had some steam to let off, some venom to loose; there would be no harm, no foul, if the frustrated monarch threw it his way. He still wasn't going anywhere.

"You think you're Romeo and Juliet, like her grandparents did? Yes, I realise you know the story," he said calmly when Toby's brows lifted. "It was I that wanted the first Giulia, and she chose Kyri." He bent to pet Puck for a moment. "I was hurt over the loss, but Hellenia was almost destroyed. The family factions following Kyri's defection gave the Orakis dynasty an opportunity to foment trouble. Decades of violence followed, thousands perished. The Marandis dynasty almost disappeared."

Toby stilled. Whatever he'd expected the King to say, it hadn't been this. "Charlie told me about the threat of war," he said quietly.

The King nodded. "I know it's hard on you. I've been there. But if I hadn't stayed, if I hadn't married a suitable woman and had sons, what would be left of Hellenia?"

The King's selfless duty filled Toby with compassion. "If it helps, I think they were deeply distressed by the fallout from their choice. They always watched the international news, and when anything about this region showed suffering they'd head to their room and talk for hours."

The King sighed and shrugged. "They could have come home. It was his father that disowned him, not me. I would have welcomed them back."

The story unfolding before him was the other side of the truth, the reality behind what he'd always seen as the most romantic story he knew. "I understand how hard it must be for you to hear this, but the man I knew was endlessly unselfish and kind. I'll always be grateful for the wonderful grandfather I knew. And Yiayia was the core of the family," he said, voice gentle. "Giulia is her grandmother's child—a Friday's child, loving and giving."

"Yes." A smile hovered on the corners of the King's lined mouth. "Our Giulia is just like her, shy and wise, dedicated to the people she loves. And she's needed here."

"She's also her grandmother's child in that she loves a quiet life," he replied, knowing he was fighting a losing battle; or maybe he'd already lost it.

"You're looking at the woman you love without seeing her." The old face held a touch of pity. "I think you've been looking after her so long that when you came here and saw what she's accomplished, how strong she is now, it shocked you."

Taken aback by the King's insight, he nodded. "And when I came here and you saw what's between us you saw a resemblance to the past."

For the first time, uncertainty shimmered in the rheumy eyes; the words and tone lacked his customary acerbity. "If she leaves, she'll hate herself for turning her back on her brother and her people to marry a man unquestionably beneath her."

The truth in that shook Toby, but he refused to show it. "You couldn't control Papou and Yiayia fifty-five years ago. You can't control Giulia's heart and decision by decree, by force, or by inventing death threats against me." The King's face turned ashen, confirmation of what he'd suspected. "You might force her to stay here with your fabricated death threats against me, but her heart is already turning from you."

"So be it, then. I will do what I must for Hellenia." The shrewd eyes held his. "It's obvious you think you have some ace up your sleeve, boy. Just say it."

He'd never have a better opening than this, and he told the King the secret he'd been holding for half his life.

Five minutes later he left the room as quietly as he'd come, feeling as blank, as devastated, as he had the day Dr Evans had told him he couldn't give Giulia his heart.

Nothing would change the facts. He was never going to be good enough for the woman who owned his very soul. He could never marry her. Never.

The next night

"This is fun."

Dressed in the simplest jeans she had in her overcrowded wardrobe and a thick, woolly pullover in her favourite shade of wine-red, her hair tumbling around her face, her skin bathed in moonlight, Giulia was exquisite. Toby caught his breath every time he looked at her. She was smiling as they lay sprawled on a makeshift picnic blanket, his bed blanket.

He'd come knocking on her secret door, as he did every night, and now they lay beneath the cool night sky in their secret dell where a fickle breeze tossed the clouds and stars around and a crackling fire gave the illusion of warmth and intimacy.

He'd set it all up hours before, bringing the blanket and sack of picnic food he'd bought at the village of Arpagos today. He'd also brought a flask of her favourite hot chocolate, a couple of hurricane lamps, and had set stones and wood in a circle for a rough fireplace. She'd gasped in delight when she'd seen it, and her thank-you hug had led to a kiss so hot it had almost made them forget the picnic.

Toby smiled and leaned over to put a third piece of home-made fruit cake in her mouth before he kissed her: the best way to ensure she didn't protest at the food. She rarely did when they were alone together, especially when she was in her beloved outdoors. "My peasant princess," he teased, and kissed her again. "Such low tastes."

She chewed and swallowed the cake, smiling, her fingers

learning the shape of his dimples, tracing the line of his jaw. "I always wanted to touch you like this," she murmured, glowing, her shining eyes stress free.

He might never be good enough for her, but she still needed him, and the lower-class fireman fought the man in love on a minute-to-minute basis.

"You were always welcome to," he murmured back, loving the way she made him tingle and ache from head to foot with wonderful, agonised desire.

It had been painful enough before, sensing but never knowing the sensual woman he'd always believed was slumbering inside her: it had been like being able to view paradise from behind prison walls. But now she'd shown him her passion he felt like a walking bushfire, in a constant state of burning, the high wind of her touch fanning the flame, and it was made stronger by being forbidden.

Oh, it was exciting to have their desire always in the subtext of their words, in every hidden look she gave him: *Come to me tonight.*

But every kiss awoke the old longings, crushed his noble decision to let her stay in Hellenia. This delicious affair in hiding wasn't right, wasn't enough—not with his beautiful Giulia—and it hurt that she didn't know how she felt beyond wanting him sexually. It hurt that, not even knowing the truth, she'd still put Hellenia above him.

"You look as if you need another kiss." She fell back on the blanket and pulled him down for a deep kiss.

Soon she was moaning and arching up to fuse their bodies. Her hands slipped under his windcheater, caressing his skin urgently, frantically, and the kiss went on and on. He couldn't stop it, and she sure as hell couldn't. She couldn't keep her hands off him when they were alone. Night after night they met in secret, talking and kissing, the passion ripping to life with a glance. The moment he opened the door to her room, or she came to his room, she'd bolt into his arms, greedy for his hands, mouth and body.

It was everything he'd ever wanted; it was so right…and so wrong.

He tore his mouth from hers, almost giving in again when he saw her sleepy eyes so dark with desire, her lips swollen. "Tell me, Giulia," he rasped. "Tell me now, and we'll make love all night."

Shutdown, turn-off. From adorable, addictive passion, she seemed a thousand miles from him, staring at him as if he'd betrayed her somehow.

He sighed and rolled off her, wishing he knew how to right old wrongs, how to make her see how lovely she was to him, how irresistible. "Let's talk."

"About what? How beautiful I am to you?" She sighed.

The tone told him not to go there, but suddenly he'd had enough of not going there, of never telling her what she needed to know, of her never saying the words he'd give his life to hear. He was tired of walking on eggshells around her damaged self-esteem, when it didn't seem to help. "It's a good start."

Her face turned pale and sad. "Repeating words by rote doesn't work, Toby. It's only good for the times tables. You should know that by now."

He leaned over her, looking in her eyes. "You're hurting me, Giulia."

She blinked and opened her mouth, but nothing came out.

He got to his feet and turned to the fire to tend it; he couldn't look at her as he said the words he'd kept locked inside for a decade, but they came out all wrong, filled with bitterness and pain. "You're ripping the heart from my chest. Damn it, you've been my best friend for years—how could you *use* me like I'm your kept man, treating me as if I'm not enough, when you have to know I'm in love with you?"

The silence felt stricken, and yet he felt the doubt shimmering from her like the moonlight bathing her in its radiance. He didn't speak. For once he refused to fill the silence for her. He stirred the coals of the little fire, waiting.

"You want me to bring us out into the open?" she asked, her voice quivering. "Charlie told you at the wedding that, now I've publicly accepted the role of princess, I can't renounce my position without the agreement of the King and the House of Hereditary Lords, didn't he? And that I didn't know it until the night we kissed?"

"Yes," he said slowly, feeling like a fool. He'd been punishing her for a rejection she didn't even know about.

Knowing what was coming, and that he deserved it, he waited.

"So you know that, by law, I can't just go home with you. They all want and believe they need me here. And I *am* needed here, Toby. You've seen it. The people need me to stay. The women and children believe I'm their advocate. They trust me not to let them down."

He picked up some pebbles beside the blanket and began tossing them at a fairy-seat, knocking the moss off in short, savage blows. "I know."

"So, why are you here with me? Why did you try to be more than my friend that first night in the passage, even here tonight, knowing I no longer have a choice to make?" she said, sounding as hurt as he had before. "Do you want us to disappear like Papou and Yiayia did? It's not so easy these days, nor so romantic. We're in the electronic age, Toby. Our faces have been plastered across the world—yours as well as mine. Will you give up your job and life in Australia to be with me? Can you think of a way to become a high lord or a prince so we can bring this out into the open?"

Having seen the constant hoops Charlie had had to jump through to make his people and the current king happy—

having seen Max forcibly engaged to one woman after another, with no say in it—Toby shuddered at the thought.

"No," he muttered. "But I waited ten years to be with you, Giulia, and I wanted my chance."

"Try fourteen years," she said wearily, her eyes dark, remote. "Unfortunately, this is all I have to give. And you're the one who said whatever I want from you is mine. Right now I need time-out."

He didn't turn or look at her, didn't speak. He knew her, knew when she had something to say, and silence helped her think.

"You know what life's like for me. It's a privilege and honour to be able to help a country rebuild itself. But instead of my biggest daily decisions being what to add to the year-end concert or what to make for dinner, I'm deciding how to split funds that need to go a hundred ways. Instead of thinking about where we'll go on the weekend, I'm thinking over which destroyed town or abused woman is most worthy of my help. Instead of standing under a spotlight on a small stage in the backblocks of Sydney, I'm standing in front of lines of begging or grateful people, or smiling for the media. On my days off I'm being pressured to decide who to marry—Max, Orakis or one of the Hereditary Lords' sons that keep showing up wherever I go. Marriage to a commoner is apparently an act of treason for me, unless you magically become acceptable. Even renouncing my position is an act the King can call treason if he wishes."

He almost burned his hand putting twigs in the fire when she tossed the word "treason" in his lap like that. Giulia was putting herself in danger every time she touched him—and yet still she'd come to him.

Giulia kept talking as if she hadn't thrown an emotional bomb at him. "I spent most of my life being ordinary, invisible to the world. Now I'm this, and everything I do is under scrutiny. Every decision affects the lives of others. I'd hoped for a little time-out with you, my best friend and lover, without making yet another life-changing decision. But after a week I'm hurting you because I can't tell you what you want to hear, because I can't choose you over everything else. Once I would have been so proud to be your girl, Toby, but you choose now to tell me…" She shrugged, the way she always did when she didn't know what to say without hurting him. "You say you love me, but is it love when you're demanding something I don't have to give you?"

She spoke with a bone-deep weariness that shook him. He'd known all this, had worried over her fatigue and stress, so why hadn't he seen it, understood her as he always had before?

I gave unconditionally before, because she was always mine unconditionally. I hate not being good enough, and I resent sharing her with the world. I wanted her to turn her back on duty and conscience and the fate of eight-million people, all for me.

He felt small, mean and petty. His aspirations and dreams of personal happiness were life-shaking to one man, not eight million.

So he said, "I'm not asking for anything from you but faith, Giulia—faith in yourself, in your beauty and desirability in my eyes."

The long silence was broken only by the crackling of the fire and the rustling of the wind in the leaves high above. "As I said, I can't give you what I don't have."

He turned to her. She was sitting jack-knifed, arms around her knees, her face downward to the earth, looking small and lonely. "Still?" he asked huskily.

Her lips sucked in, she gave a short, jerking nod. "I don't doubt you love me. But the rest—are they words my best friend's using because I'm losing weight? Are you saying you want me because you want to save me again? How can I believe you when you only say the words when you feed me, or feel guilty over what you believe you've done to me?"

Startled by the depth of her insight, he rocked back on his heels. "What would it take to make you believe me?"

She shrugged, staring at the ground, at the fire, anywhere but at him. "Maybe if I'd had one man interested in me before I became sister to a future king, if someone thought I was pretty before I became Europe's last single princess, if you'd shown me you wanted me before now... But it's too late for might-have-beens." She smiled at him, heartbreaking in her courage and sacrifice, refusing to lay blame. *"C'est la vie."*

He knew this was going to amount to the equivalent of shooting himself in the foot, but it had to be said. "Almost all the single guys at the station have the hots for you, Giulia. Dozens of other men have wanted you. Why do you think big brothers kept coming to pick up the girls from ballet class—for the joy it gave their sisters?"

She frowned, but kept her gaze on the fire. "Nice try, but it's not going to work. They were all nice to me, but not one asked me out."

Here we go. Now he had to pull out that shotgun and aim it right between his eyes. He knew better than to touch her as he made the confession. "The only reason none of them asked you out was because I was always there, acting like your boyfriend—and if that didn't work I scared them off."

"What?" She looked up now, her eyes bewildered. "Why would you do something like that?"

Like a condemned man, he saw his life flash in front of his eyes as he searched for a way to make it sound better, gave up and told the truth. "I couldn't stand the thought of anyone touching you but me. I loved you too damn much, waited years for you. I wasn't going to lose you to some guy who wouldn't love and appreciate you like I did. Like I do," he finished hoarsely, his heart screaming for his beautiful best friend, his love, to understand.

She was silent for a long time, and he felt every single thud of his heart as he waited for her answer.

"So essentially what you're telling me is that, while you enjoyed a normal life with flirtations and relationships, had all the fun and made all the mistakes of the normal human, you left me alone for ten years wondering what was so wrong with me that no man even saw me as attractive?" she asked, her tone almost conversational. "That's your idea of loving me?"

He sat on the blanket as his legs gave way. She'd just shown him the last ten years through her eyes.

After saving her life from a disease that was all based on self-image, he'd left her alone, feeling ugly and unwanted, because he hadn't spoken. Though he'd dated, even slept with other women when he'd lost hope with her, he'd stopped any man coming near her because she was *his,* because he'd burned with near-insane jealousy at the thought of any other man touching her. While she'd gone through the torment of knowing where he was and what he was doing with those other women, he hadn't been able to put himself through the same.

How she'd remained strong enough to not fall into anorexic patterns all these years, he had no idea. How she was surviving royal life without running, screaming back to Australia was still a mystery to him.

The King had been right about her. Max had seen everything in her that he'd been blind to. The real woman beneath the one he'd chosen to see was strong, wise and courageous, far more than he'd ever been during any fire.

Did he know her at all?

She sat there, watching him with no accusation in her eyes. She knew him, knew he was accusing himself enough for them both.

"There's nothing I can say," he mumbled eventually.

"No," she agreed, still impassive.

"They were real, Giulia. Those guys, the ones at the station. Hell, Sean and Jack and Tim always fought over who you'd smiled at the most when you came to visit—at least until I was around," he told her, frantic to find a way to fix his latest mistake with her. "Remember they all came to the local production of *Giselle,* and you thought it was to laugh at me being Loys? They came to see you. Ask Charlie if you can't believe me," he added, knowing at last that he hadn't earned her trust after all these years.

Throwing out the anorexic rulebook had saved her ten years ago. But, smug, thinking he knew her better than anyone, he'd thrown out the more commonsense advice such as letting Giulia fly when she was ready, allowing her to find her own life. No book knew what Giulia needed—he did.

But he now saw the truth: it had never been about what *she'd* needed. He'd done it to keep her with him because he needed her, because he was scared stupid that, if he let some other man near her, she might need them more.

He felt sick, realising the King and Max had been right. He'd never treated Giulia with the respect and dignity of an adult free to make her own choices.

"Thank you," she said after a while, with a politeness that put miles of distance between them. "It was kind of you to tell me that."

"But you don't believe it, do you?"

She opened her mouth and closed it. She didn't have to answer.

"We should go back in. I have a big day tomorrow, and so do you," he said, cursing a brain so scrambled he knew anything he said now would make it worse.

She nodded, and started putting food in the rucksack. "Thank you for my lovely picnic, Toby. It was, um, nice to relax after a hard day."

And he'd blown it again, putting his needs before hers, and those of millions of others who needed her.

He couldn't tell her about the real source of his so-called death threats now. How would it change her mind when he was only "time-out" to her? And no wonder at that. He'd been her first kiss, the kiss she should have had at sixteen. He'd had the normal rounds of first kisses and sweet, innocent dates, but he'd denied them to her.

He'd even ruined this time every woman ought to be able to treasure by bringing shame on their assignations, and by his demands that she put him first. And even now, he'd demanded she overcome the pain he'd inflicted on her, change the ruin of her self-esteem, and see how much he loved her anyway.

He'd spent years trying to love the way Giulia did—the way all the Costas did, giving without expectation—and still he was a scrapping, grabbing Winder, wanting more than he had, never able to let go of what he saw as his right, his due.

As they headed back to the cave, he said what he had to. "I think you should date." Every word came out gravelly, as if spoken through broken glass. "Max is a good guy. Some of the Lords' sons are decent too—and it's obvious a few of them really like you." He named the men he thought had a chance of making themselves worthy of her, even though a streak of pain went through his left side, as if his heart squeezed out its protest in blood.

After hearing him out, she said quietly, "You might be right, but I'm not ready for it yet." And though she smiled at him, he knew she meant: *They don't want me...*

He felt like Judas, betraying her with his kiss.

"Why don't you hit me?" he demanded, drowning under the weight of her sweetness, the regal bearing that was born in her. From little Lia, holding her hand out to him saying, "Come and live with us," to the princess walking beside him in her jeans and pullover, she'd always been so high above him, he didn't deserve even to look at her. "You deserve to take a swing at me for being so damned selfish all those years."

She lifted one shoulder. "You were anything but selfish, Toby—and it wouldn't change those years anyway. They'll still exist."

In other words, *the damage is done and there's nothing you can do to fix it.*

In the cave, she turned to him, her lovely, sleepy eyes shimmering with sadness and regret and half a lifetime of trusting love shattered that she was trying so hard to hide for his sake. "Don't blame yourself, Toby. You saved my life. I've never doubted how much you love me. And if I'd spoken, tried again…"

"Don't try to absolve me, Giulia, I couldn't stand it," he said hoarsely. And with the last word, he plunged into a secret passage as dark as his soul at this moment.

CHAPTER EIGHT

A week later

TOBY had known it was only a matter of time before Orakis made a blunder. All he'd had to do was wait for the spoiled lord's anger to build high enough.

Two nights ago Giulia had tired of Orakis's calls, extolling his own virtues. Politely, but with a firmness that told everyone listening in that he had no hope of winning her, she'd said she was too busy at present to take his daily calls. No, she wouldn't have a private dinner with him either.

Giulia had shuddered when she'd told him about it later, as she recounted listening to the icy silence before Orakis had hung up the phone. But Toby felt the ripple of inner excitement. It was time.

After Giulia had left the small town where she'd opened a new refuge Toby had waited two miles down the road with a fully equipped truck, his security contingent and a few retired firefighters.

It was almost two hours later before the explosion came but it looked like Chinese New Year, a burst of light and colour shooting up into the afternoon sky.

The team swung into action. "Nobody's going to die today,"

he told the men in grim promise. "We fight back—not dirty, but *clever.* Stick to the plan."

They all nodded. They knew what he wanted them to do, and were ready to meet resistance if necessary. They shoved on their masks and ran in.

And Toby knew there wouldn't be a fight. The two men sent to set the fire were trapped beneath a beam that had crashed down on them with the first explosion, and were screaming for help.

He sent two experienced men in to check the rest of the place. Then he ran into the back of the building where the walls were beginning to topple, the roof sliding sideways.

The beam that had fallen on them was a supporting one. These two were idiots, not even knowing enough to get out before the explosion. Grimly he shoved a massive broken shard of the beam under the stairs to keep them up until his men cleared the building, and went to work to pull out Dumb and Dumber. He had two, three minutes at the most, before the fire got too close and these dopes would die.

"Hang on, I'll get you out," he yelled in English as he used a battery-powered chainsaw to break up the thick slab of wood, so there'd be no sparks. He hoped it wasn't yet common knowledge that the Prince's old friend spoke Hellenican Greek like a native.

"Lord Orakis will be furious with us for this," one of them muttered to the other, in such breathless pain Toby knew he had at least one crushed rib. "But he did tell us to break this beam first!"

Toby tossed aside half the beam. "I won't be long now," he said in English.

"What if they don't get us out before the accelerant in the cellar explodes?" the other panted, ignoring Toby completely. "It can't be long now."

Toby tossed aside the second half of the beam. The young guys in his team were working on shoving pieces of steel to keep things up for now. "I'm just about done, so I'll have you out in time, but thank you for the information," he said politely in their language, and Orakis's men gasped.

He checked them for spinal injury, cleared them for movement and carried one out, calling to one of the guys to take the other. Both men were totally silent now, probably weighing up their options to avoid prison time.

Toby and the other firefighter handed Orakis's men to the paramedics. "Request police surveillance in the hospital for these two. They're the arsonists. Search them—they may also have evidence that the fire was ordered by Lord Orakis," he said briefly and, to the beat of cheering townspeople, he ran back in to find the accelerant and other traces of evidence before the building collapsed.

Checking the stairs for signs of hazardous materials before he got the accelerant out, he heard a strained voice from below. "Toby. Toby Winder…"

Toby blinked and yelled, *"Max?"*

Lia walked past liveried servants, holding the doors open for her, after returning from an afternoon tea for charity. Last night had been a state dinner.

She sighed in relief. She actually had tomorrow off, and she was planning to do some serious sleeping in until Charlie and Jazmine called for their updates.

The King knew about the calls; everyone did. Everyone listened in, wanting to see how things were going.

But, though she tried, she couldn't bring herself to date. Max was handsome, suave and charming, with a heart as untouched by her as hers was by him. They'd always be friends, but nothing more. Lately she'd had some calls from Georgiou, the son of the Earl of Conroi. He was young and eager, and good-looking in a dark, intense way, and looked at her with restrained hunger. Toby was right—Georgiou did really like her—but all she wanted to do was pat him on the head. He seemed so *young*.

She headed for her room, intending to ask her maid for a peppermint tea. All the rich cakes and biscuits at the afternoon tea didn't sit well in her stomach.

A commotion from the eastern wing made her frown. There were people striding back and forth, and people in white coats snapping orders. She looked through the balconies to the front gate; a mass of headlights and flashing lights told her the press was here in force.

"What's going on?" she asked her security detail, who followed her in silence. When the man and woman refused to answer, she snapped, sick to death of everyone hiding things from her. "If you don't tell me, I'll ask the press outside for news."

The woman's jaw tightened, but the man clearly hesitated. She pressed her advantage. "I'm sure King Angelis will be very glad of your discretion when I walk out to the gate and ask one of the press while the cameras are still rolling."

The woman still didn't answer, so she turned to the man. He gave a short nod. "Mr Winder was injured in a fire at one of your refuges, Your Highness."

"Toby," Lia gasped, turned and ran down the hall.

Several royal staff blocked the way. "I'm sorry, Your Highness, but nobody is to enter Mr Winder's room but medical staff."

At that, the fury, a low-burning match in her heart, turned to a blaze. She turned to her male security-detail. "Find me an unopened jar of honey, an unopened bottle of pure aloe-juice, Vaseline gauze, bandages, and tape instead of butterfly clips. Now!"

The man, accustomed to the voice of command, turned and ran.

She headed straight for the King's sitting room. "Let me

past," she snapped to the servants at the doors of King Angelis's sitting room.

She opened the door to the King's day room without waiting for them to announce her. The King looked up from the papers he was reading, seeming unperturbed by her entrance. "I gather you've discovered the boy's injury. Sit down, Giulia, and we'll talk."

Lia remained standing. "I want you to remove the orders not to let me into Toby's room, Your Majesty. I know how to treat him."

The gap between them was evident in the way she'd called him "Your Majesty," yet the King's face didn't harden. "You have to be reasonable, child. How would it look if you—?"

"I don't care how it looks," she interrupted brutally. "Make your choice, sire."

"You won't call me Theo Angelis now?" His voice and face were sad, old.

Her heart gave an unwilling tug, but she repressed it. He was using her soft heart to get his way. "I can't love a man forcing me into something that revolts me. Papou would never have hurt me that way."

"No doubt," the King sneered. "If you want to see your lover, why don't you sneak in via the secret passage, as you've been doing for the last couple of weeks?"

She maintained her stance in the face of his anger. "I won't hide our friendship—and I won't use my royal privilege to keep my dearest friend as my secret lover."

A wave of colour stained the old man's face. His jaw jutted.

"I will go to Toby openly to treat his wounds. I don't care if I have to create a scene or go through the press to do it."

The King's jaw worked for a moment. "Fine, put him in danger. It suits me." He picked up the phone and snapped the order.

Lia turned and walked out without another word. She

strode up the stairs, turned right and went into Toby's wing. The security detail parted this time.

Toby was leaning back on a gurney brought in as medical staff worked on him. He was pale; his shoulder and hands were draped with sterile padding.

"Out," she snapped at the medical staff, crossing the room to him.

Toby's eyes opened and he grinned, lifting his brows at her peremptory tone. "Come in, Your Highness."

The medical staff bowed as they protested, but she'd had it with listening to everyone else. "Don't patronise me. I've been a princess for four months and a fireman's sister for ten years. I have my advanced First Aid, updated every year, and an EMT certificate. I've probably treated almost as many burn injuries on my brother, Toby and other members of his station as you have patients in hospitals." She moved to the trolley. "Good, Vaseline gauze and bandages. Don't give him straight penicillin, he's allergic, and he reacts badly to the antibiotic cream and glucose-based antiseptic. He can only take a broad-based oral antibiotic, which is useless in this case, unless he becomes infected—which he won't. He never does with my treatment. Now please, everyone, out before someone gives him staph. Leave the trolley."

Toby grinned again once the door closed behind the multitudes. "Did you mean to turn me on with that tirade? You're as sexy as sin when you're giving everyone hell for my sake."

"I doubt the King agreed when he tried to lock me out of here." Still feeling the hot blush on her cheeks, she laughed and, after braiding her hair back and washing her hands thoroughly, began opening packets. "When necessity drives, right?"

"Obviously you felt the necessity, or you wouldn't be starting World War Three for my sake. Think the King will come in, all guns blazing, to see if I can seduce you without my hands?"

Though he was still laughing, she heard the deep thread of pain beneath. "Be quiet and let me see your hands. One of the staff will be back with the aloe and honey soon." Once she had gloves on, she lifted the sterile covers and inspected his shoulder beneath one of the plastic-backed sterile sheets. "There are some second-degree burns here." She had to work fast or he'd need those antibiotics by morning. "Did they finish cleaning all the wounds?"

He closed his eyes. "Apart from a few splinters they found in my hands."

She checked them out. "A *few* splinters? There's over two-dozen here." She took the first six ampoules of saline and ran them under hot water. Water just cooler than lukewarm, she'd learned, helped bring the splinters to the surface on burned skin, and didn't shock the damaged flesh as much. "So what did you do to get this many?" she asked when she returned with a calmness she'd never really felt in treating Charlie or Toby—but keeping serene helped them to relax.

"Fallen beam on two of Orakis's goons. I couldn't get it off them with the gloves on. I burned my shoulder while I was pulling Max out—and my hands burned getting the barrel of flame-accelerant out before it exploded. Then the place started collapsing, and…" He shrugged, and she nodded. She knew the story; she'd heard similar tales over and over in the past ten years.

"Max was there?" she asked, burning with curiosity. "Why? Is he all right?"

"He has concussion, some blurred vision. Luckily he re-gained consciousness in time to call to me." Toby's face showed no expression. "He was there because, like me, he sus-pected Orakis would torch the place. He saw the goons place the accelerant in the cellar, and they hit him and tied him up. When they tried to run, the supporting beam went, trapping them."

"Ah." She grinned at him. "I see I've been kept out of the loop with your most recent rounds of dangerous antics, dear friend. If you want these splinters removed with as few ouches as possible, I suggest you expound the tale."

He grinned; his eyes were so warm she wanted to swim in them. "I think I've done it, Giulia. I found proof that Orakis is behind the fire attacks on the buildings we've set up for our projects in Hellenia—yours, mine and Charlie's. I found a barrel full of top-grade accelerant set with a timer in the cellar beside Max. And believe it or not, Orakis's men kept the written instructions on them. The police have them in custody. They talked about Orakis knowing of the arson before they realised I could speak Hellenican. I told the police the King would have their names and the station in question, in case of any 'accidental' escapes."

Lia blinked. He'd said "I've done it" as though he'd been seeking a way to bring Orakis down for a while.

Then her heart filled and overflowed. Of course he had; he wouldn't allow her life to be dominated by that man. Toby had devoted so many years to her health and happiness, she was amazed she hadn't realised before that he'd do this—risking his life to free her from any harm or threat was just what he did.

She bent and kissed his cheek, aching to touch him, not as friend or would-be nurse, but as a lover. "Thank you, Toby, thank you."

But he frowned. "Don't thank me. I did what I had to do."

"For me," she said softly, kissing him full on the lips this time, lingering until his mouth softened and he kissed her back. "Now it's my turn to help you."

"How can you still want to kiss me after everything I've done to you?" he murmured, filled with self-recrimination. "How can you forgive me for hurting you all those years?"

"Ah, Toby," she whispered, and the aching intensified to kiss him again. "I know you didn't mean to hurt me—and don't you know I'd forgive you anything?"

His eyes darkened but, as he was about to speak, a knock came on the door. She called out, her voice wobbly, "Come in."

Her Secret Service man came in with a large paper bag.

She checked out the contents and smiled. "I can't believe you actually found Manuka honey, Rob. It's the purest honey there is, and full of natural antibiotics."

Rob smiled back, and she knew it was because she'd called him by his name.

"Can you stand at the door and make certain no one comes in? All those people around open wounds is a recipe for infection. Mr Winder's allergic to penicillin."

"Certainly, Your Highness." Rob left the room, closing the door behind him.

Lia opened all the things she'd need, and then washed her hands again. Then she returned to Toby. Seeing his dirty, grimed face, inhaling the pungent smell of smoke, knowing what he'd endured for her sake, she ached and burned with the need to speak, to thank him, to tell him...

What? If she told him how she felt, he'd never leave and a war could start; he could die.

She closed her eyes, pressed her lips together, then nodded in silent resolution. After all he'd done for her for so many years right up until today, she owed him so much. She'd give him the words he'd asked for, if nothing else.

I am the most beautiful...

But she choked on them, even in her mind. She'd spent eleven years thinking the worst of her dark looks, her quiet, home-loving personality. But though her long-held habit of silence had been breaking ever since Toby had first kissed her, this was the biggest of them all. Believing in herself after all these years... She realised she'd rather tell him she was hopelessly besotted with her best friend than say words she couldn't make herself believe.

"How long have you been planning to bring Orakis down?" she asked as she cleaned the burns around the splinters.

"Since you told me you might have to marry him." He sounded surprised she'd have to ask. "His moves were obvious to a trained fireman, and nobody else seemed to want to take him on. Though Max surprised me," he added with a grin. "He's not the pampered nancy boy I thought he was. He can combat-swim, fly a plane and track through a forest without leaving a trace of his presence."

"I'm sure he can." All those skills were on her future agenda as well. Lia laughed at his irreverent terminology for the Grand Duke with a closed mouth, to protect his open wounds, and got back to the subject. "You're crazy, taking on Orakis like that. Does nothing frighten you, Winder?"

She felt his intense blue gaze on her. "The thought of living my life without you terrifies me."

Her lungs seized up—her heart pounded hard and fast as it always did when he said things like that, making it nearly impossible to speak—but she forced words out. "Me too. I can't stand to *think*—" She shook her head. "Now look at me, I'm shaking. I can't get your splinters out if I'm emotional. So behave."

"For now," he said, with quiet intent. "When you're done, beloved, you *are* going to finish that sentence."

She almost dropped the sterile tweezers.

His eyes met hers, dark, serious. "We're out of time, Giulia."

Moved to her soul, she managed to smile at him. "Yes," she agreed, her voice off-kilter again, so filled with longing he had to know, had to see it.

It took almost an hour to bathe Toby's hands and remove the splinters from the burned flesh, dress all his wounds and make him comfortable. While she worked, he told her he'd been sure Orakis would overreach himself before long. By making plans that allowed two unimportant minions to die in the fire, by sending in dummies who'd tried to kill the Grand Duke, Orakis had unravelled his own power—or Toby had done so, by the simple act of saving all three men's lives. Grovellingly grateful to the man who'd saved them, wanting vengeance on Orakis, his minions had agreed to make full confessions in exchange for reduced sentences.

"Even if Orakis gets off, I gave a statement to the press," he finished, sounding incredibly tired. "Not only has he lost any chance with you, he's going to lose the King's silence and the goodwill of the people by torching two refuge centres set up by their beloved princess. Max also made a statement."

"Orakis ordered the fires, knowing his own people would die." Lia shuddered in horror as she finished binding his shoulder. She pulled on a clean pair of sterile gloves to rub a mixture of lanolin and aloe into the minor burns. "How could he do that?"

"How anyone else does in the world," he murmured, breathing deeply, relaxing with the gentle touch of her palms on his skin. "It's called collateral damage. Sacrifices are required for what they believe is the best thing for the country. They usually don't require the sacrifice of those who'll benefit most, though."

She felt something inside her turn very still and tense. It was as if her whole body was listening to the words Toby hadn't aimed at her.

A sacrifice for the country. In the King's eyes, in the eyes of the Lords, *she* was that. And while she was honoured to be their princess and do what she could for Hellenia, what she was sacrificing was her future happiness, her heart. She had to give up happiness for the sake of birth and blue blood, a centuries-old tradition invented by those in power, and it hadn't stopped one minute of war.

But her sacrifice was also for the sake of Toby's life.

Her hands moved over his skin in the soothing touch she'd given him whenever he'd been burned, accepting the sacrifice she must make.

She went to the door and asked Rob to bring a wash bowl. An eager crowd pressed forward but she closed the door in their faces, locking it until Rob returned.

She filled the bowl with warm, soapy water and a facecloth, picked up a towel and returned to Toby. He was breathing deeply. Careful to avoid his bandages and burns she'd covered with sterile gauze, she washed the smoke grime from his face and body. Her own body thudded with need at the intimacy of the touch, but his need was greater. Her soapy hands moved over his chest, stomach and arms, rinsing him with the washcloth and patting him dry with a towel, her mind and heart filled with beautiful, impossible visions, and her body...

He groaned as she cleaned his exposed legs and feet. "Thank you, Giulia." He sounded hoarse with repressed sensuality.

"Hair next," she whispered, throat thick. She lowered the gurney, rinsed the bowl and added fresh water. When she returned, he'd moved to the end of the gurney. She made a makeshift table from the trolley and shampooed his hair, trying to be gentle, but she knew her fingers moved with the same pounding pulse of sexuality that controlled her because she was near him. She didn't dare ask if his groans were of relief at losing the hated smoky smell or because he was as aroused as she.

By the time she'd towelled his hair touch-dry, she didn't know which of them had undergone the sweetest torture. Unable to stop herself, she bent and kissed his lips, slow and lingering.

He opened his eyes and smiled, his eyes filled with the same anguished desire as hers. "Please tell me that was less of a thank-you for today's efforts, or even in much-needed forgiveness for all my stupidity and selfishness with you, and more that you're sexually overwrought by touching my half-naked body."

She chuckled, bent and kissed him again. "How about all of the above?"

"I'll take it." He sat up on the gurney, got to his feet, smiled with that slow-dawning sensuality and made a beckoning motion with his bandaged hand. "Tell me, my Giulia," he murmured, close, so close. "Say the words."

"I can't," she whispered back, swaying against him. "I know you love me. I know you find me…attractive enough. But the rest…" She shook her head hopelessly, wanting to cry. He'd just risked his life to save her from marrying Orakis. Why couldn't she *believe?*

"Then I'll wait." His eyes were like a sunlit morning; his dimples flashed as he smiled at her. "If I have to wait the rest of my life, I'll prove it to you somehow.

"Now, what were you going to say to me before?" he went on, as if he hadn't turned her world spinning the other way with those simple words.

Through a throat so filled with a pounding pulse she could barely speak, her voice came, a strangled croak. "I can't stand the thought of life without you."

"That's disappointing, beloved. I knew that already." With his bandaged hand, he drew hers to his mouth and kissed it. "What you *ought* to have said is something about how much you want me, that all that washing of my naked chest, stomach and back drove you as wild with desire as it did me."

How could she be shaking with half-crazed want and smothering laughter at the same time? "I do, and it did," she managed to say.

"Good," he growled softly, moving his hips against hers with luscious intent, and she moaned. "Now, tell me you want me. I've waited years to hear it." He smiled at her panicked silence, bent and kissed her throat, slow, hot and lingering. "Then I'll start. I love being your best friend—but I also want to be your lover, Giulia." The whisper, soft and husky, seemed to come from the deepening velvet of the dusk falling outside. "For ten years I've wanted to kiss your mouth, to touch your body, to undress you and fill my hands and mouth with your beautiful breasts, to move inside you and feel you come apart in my arms."

She gasped and quivered. Her mind spun with delicious arousal, her breasts ached, and deep inside she was thudding with hot, craving want. The craving for him, him alone, that she hadn't conquered after all these years.

"*Want* you?" she cried with a wild laugh, unable to stop the dam of repressed longings bursting open. "I hunger for you. I *starve* for you. When you're near me I ache and crave; my whole body's alive and hurting to touch you, to make love with you. It's been a screaming need in my soul since you stripped off your shirt in front of me after you moved into our house, and nothing that's come between us has changed it. You're *it*, you're the one, and it's killing me inside that these few days are all we can have together!" She turned away as she asked huskily, "Why didn't you kiss me years ago? Why didn't you make love to *me* instead of all the girls you say you can't remember and I can't forget? Why didn't you give me the one thing that would have made me feel beautiful and wanted, that would have made me believe—?" A sob escaped her throat.

His arms enveloped her; gentle, bandaged hands pressed, and her head fell to his undamaged shoulder. He didn't answer the questions they both knew were rhetorical. Her arms wrapped around his waist, drinking in his skin with tiny movements of her palms and fingers. She breathed in the still-just-smoky, hot scent of him, so wonderful to her because it was him.

"I warned you not to make me let it all out," she whispered after a long time. "I said too much."

"It was perfect." He softly kissed her hair. "I've waited ten years for you to tell me what you feel for me. You made it worth every moment."

There was nothing to say in response. "I love you" seemed almost trite after all she'd said. So she turned her face, pressing a kiss to his shoulder.

Then the hunger filled her, and the slow, hot kisses she poured all over his throat, undamaged shoulder and chest only fuelled the need. Aching to her fingertips, her hands roamed his skin; she turned him round and kissed his back, caressing his stomach, so aroused and filled with need for him that nothing else mattered. The craving inside her was pain; she couldn't stop.

Then she felt the slight tremors running through his tough, strong body—and knew he wasn't moving or speaking because he was exhausted and in need of pain relief and couldn't bring himself to tell her. Love filled her and overflowed. Always putting her first...

She led him to the big, carved-oak bed at the end of the room and lifted the covers. "Lie down, Toby. I'll ask the doctor to come in."

"No. I don't want anyone else." He lay down and held out his arms. "Just you. Even if it's only for a few minutes before the old guy busts us."

She smiled at his cheeky terminology for His Majesty, crossed to the left side of the bed, lying down beside him, snuggling into his chest. "I'll have to go soon anyway," she said quietly. "I need to go check on Max."

He stilled. "I see."

"I'm sorry," she said, feeling wretched. "But he's been so good to me. He risked his life today too, and I..."

"I know. It's not your fault." The words were weary.

"It's never going to be the same for us, is it? Our friendship won't be the same."

She felt the sigh come from deep inside him. "No." He tipped her face up to his with a bandaged hand, his jaw taut, showing the physical discomfort it cost him. "Did I put you through this kind of torment when I went on those stupid dates?"

She looked into his eyes, saw the anger and useless regret, the hopeless wanting and all the pain, and choked out the words: "Every time."

"Bloody idiot," he muttered. "If I'd told you…"

"If I'd told you," she sighed. But what-ifs were useless. She'd accepted her duty and privilege; to renounce her position would make an impossible situation for Charlie and Jazmine, and put Toby's life in danger. That was the reality she had to deal with.

"There has to be a way for us to be together, Giulia. It can't end like this, after all these years. I can't stop thinking about it, trying to find a way for us."

The hard, exhausted growl made her quiver for a moment with hope—then it crashed and burned like the building today. "There is none."

"Damn it, there has to be. We can't just give up."

She looked up at him. "What is there, short of a miracle? Even if I could renounce my position, I can't live a private life now without the press making our lives a nightmare. I'll always be the Australian-born sister of Hellenia's king. You can't become a prince. The people wouldn't allow it."

Toby swore. "All this ridiculous fuss over bloodlines. If we'd married a year ago—or five—we wouldn't be in this mess."

She sighed. "I know."

She felt him withdrawing from her without moving. She understood that; the need to lock away some small part of herself every time he'd been with someone else had been her lifeline since his first date with Mandy.

"I wish…" But she couldn't finish it, couldn't wish that he'd never spoken, never kissed her. She just wished Dr Evans had never spoken to Toby.

"No matter what happens, I'll be here when you need me," he said quietly. "That's what best friends do."

"Yes," she whispered, wanting to say, "I'll be there for you too," but they both knew it was a promise she couldn't make or keep. "Sleep now." She reached up and caressed his damp hair.

When she knew he was asleep, she kissed his cheek, his mouth, so tenderly he wouldn't feel it. *I love you,* she mouthed, and slipped from the room.

CHAPTER NINE

An Uncommon Love: Princess Giulia's Best Friend Rescues Her Grand Duke From a Burning Building
National Hero: the Grand Duke Proposes Knighthood for Toby Winder
Lord Orakis Flees Hellenia in Disgrace. His People Turn Him In!

Extraordinary Meeting, House of Hereditary Lords
A week later

"FOR your services to crown and country, in the name of King Angelis and in his sickness, we knight you Sir Toby Winder." Charlie, who'd come back with Jazmine from their extended honeymoon for one day to give Toby this honour, placed the golden sword either side of Toby's shoulders with a grin. "Welcome to the nobility, Grizz," he said as, with a proud, happy smile, Jazmine placed the knight's cloak over his shoulders.

Kneeling at their feet, he winked at his old friend. "You never could handle going anywhere without me, could you?"

Charlie laughed and slapped him on the back. "It's your fault, mate. If you didn't want to become a noble, you shouldn't have saved a Grand Duke's life and taken Orakis down all in a day."

After Charlie helped him to his feet, since he still didn't have use of his hands, Toby turned and smiled at the applauding lords around him, nodding. "Talk about surreal," he muttered. He now owned lands in Charlie's region of Malascos as well as being a knight of the realm.

But it still wasn't enough to claim the hand of a princess.

With a major struggle, he smiled over at said princess. Giulia was wiping away tears as she smiled with obvious pride…and sorrow.

"A knighthood is all you can have," Charlie had said to them this morning when they'd arrived, saying it with obvious awkwardness. "Every other title in Hellenia is hereditary, mate, has been for hundreds of years. If I could make it higher…"

In other words, he'd never rise high enough to be worthy of Giulia.

He had a title, but the same wall existed. He was part of the Costa—Marandis—good fortune and love, but ten steps behind, as he'd been for fourteen years.

The reality was inescapable: if he stayed in Hellenia he'd be rich, famous and titled, but he'd still be Lancelot to her Guinevere. Looking at her now, he knew she knew it, too, and he watched her gentle heart breaking in front of him.

The next night

"There's something you need to know. Sit down, boy."

Facing the King in yet another one-sided interview, Toby knew what he had to say. The King didn't care what the media thought of his unwanted house guest; Toby had no interest in bantering words, or reiterating his protest that he'd stay as long as Giulia and Charlie needed him.

His hands were healing. Charlie and Jazmine were due back from their honeymoon in another five days. The coronation ceremony was scheduled for the second Saturday after that.

Charlie would back him up if he decided to stay. There was so much to do, and his schemes were working well. But…

You're it, you're the one.

Since the day he'd been knighted and she'd seen the look in his eyes, Giulia had withdrawn from him. She'd come to his room this morning to clean and dress his wounds, speaking to him as she had in the past: as her dear and trusted friend. She left as soon as his bandages had been changed, and she'd arranged for the King's valet to shave him, even though she'd always done so when he'd burned himself in the past.

There were no burning kisses, no uncontrollable passion. Touching had become unbearable for them both.

Crowns, palaces and knighthoods, limos and jets; duty, conscience and helping her brother; death threats and treason; he had nothing to give her but his love, and even that put a burden on her…

"You have to go home now. I've organised a jet for you, and—"

Toby frowned. The King's voice wasn't hard or abrupt, but strangely touched with sympathy. "Your Majesty, I've told you—"

"No, Toby," the King said quietly, using his name for the first time since they'd met. "This isn't about your friendship with Giulia. This time you must go home."

Toby went cold all over. "What is it, sire? What's happened?"

The next night
Sydney, Australia

As the jet landed at the part of Kingsford-Smith airport reserved for VIPs, Lia sat tensely, unmoving except for her toes tapping on the Berber carpet. Her gaze wasn't on the gorgeously lit nightline all around the harbour; it remained on the note Toby had written.

> I have to go home, Giulia. My father died. I'll try to return for Charlie and Jazmine's coronation, but if things go wrong and I can't, I wish you all a wonderful life. You know where I am if you ever need me. Give my love to Charlie.
> Toby

Tears clogged her throat. Toby's beautiful words always deserted him when he was in pain…

The King's kindness at a time when she was in deep shock had been a wonderful relief. He'd taken care of everything, not just for her, but for Toby as well.

"Toby's father passed away suddenly. The second royal-jet is waiting for you, my dear. Everything has been packed, a suite booked for each of you at the best hotel in Sydney, and your security is ready and waiting for you in Australia. Charlie and Jazmine will arrive the day after you."

As Sir Toby Winder, member of the Hellenican nobility, Toby had been sent home in one of the diplomatic jets and was staying in a five-star harbourside suite with a full contingent of security as befitted his position as best friend to a king-in-waiting. Yet he'd been sent home alone when his father had died.

She'd been at a party, where she'd met many of the young nobles the King and Lords judged worthy of her, and she'd been jaw-droppingly bored. She'd only gone to please everyone, to show she was willing to make further adjustments in her life. To leave Toby behind for the sake of royal duty.

Because she hadn't come home until after midnight, she'd missed the chance to support Toby as he'd done for her so many years; had left him alone and grieving.

The fifteen-minute drive had taken for ever, but finally she was there, and the usual rigmarole started, the bowing and gracious words. *Toby, where was he?*

At last, at last, she was in the lift, and it pinged on the top floor where there were only three massive suites. Security staff were everywhere, the head someone-or-other was ushering her to her suite.

"Please, which is Sir Toby's suite?" she asked, cutting off the man's polite talk with a gentle smile.

He knocked on the door for her, but she called out, "Toby?"

Seconds later he opened the door. He looked white and haggard; his eyes fixed on her like a starving man faced with a banquet. "Giulia?" His voice was hoarse.

"If there are security cameras inside the suite, I want them turned off," she said to the man behind her.

"You can do that yourself, Your Highness, though I would be happy to."

"It's fine. I can do it, really. Thank you again. We'll call if we need anything."

"Giulia?" Toby blinked, shaking his head as if she was a phantom. His hands touched her face, probing, wondering, as if he couldn't believe it was her. It made her want to cry.

Without a word she took him in her arms, walked him backward into the suite and closed the door behind them. When she'd turned off the cameras, she held his face in her hands. "Have you eaten? Do you want food or coffee?"

"You're here. You're here," he said, still as if he couldn't take it in, as if she was a miracle in his eyes.

"Of course I am," she said gently, moved. "How could you not know I'd come? I'd do anything for you, Toby, don't you know that yet?"

"Giulia," was all he said. His hands kept touching her face, with such unspoken reverence the knowledge came to her…a truth she should have known all along.

But now wasn't the time. "How are you feeling? How's your family?"

He shook his head, blinking as if to orientate himself. "I think they're okay. I called them. Even Mum's going to the funeral, Jonathan said. They asked me over to discuss the funeral plans, but I haven't been allowed out of here."

Shocked, Lia said, "You can't visit your family? Why?"

"They said something about the media fuss over my knighthood, and being friends with you and Charlie, and the death threats. They seem to think Australia isn't security-conscious enough. Anyone could infiltrate the press or even the funeral without proper security arrangements, apparently. So they've taken over. The King's paid for the entire shebang, even the wake." He tried to smile. "It's a good thing, since Dad didn't have insurance."

Lia was horrified. "Oh, Toby, I'm so sorry—it's because of us. Charlie's on his way, of course. We weren't going to leave you alone, but it means there'll be ASIO everywhere. If you don't want us to come…"

"Come." He buried his face in her hair. "It makes no difference. Being the best friend of a king means high security anyway, in case someone kidnaps me to get to Charlie or you."

"I'm sorry, so sorry," she choked. "When Theo Angelis told me, I didn't even think beyond that you'd need me. I didn't realise…"

"I do need you. I've been pacing like a crazy man all day without you. I want to help them, do something for Dad, but I can't. I can't even go to the damn funeral home and tell my father I'm sorry I left the family that way." His voice cracked. "I didn't even know my own father, Giulia, and it's my fault."

Holding him to her, Lia walked him to the massive lounge and sat down on his lap. "No, Toby, that's not true. They put you in an impossible position because they hated each other."

His face darkened with self-recrimination. "I could have

made it better. I didn't want to. I didn't want to be one of them. I visited them like they were in prison. I wanted to forget I was a Winder. I became one of your family and left them behind."

"You were *fifteen,* Toby, and they disowned you," she replied, trying to be gentle, but feeling fierce inside. "You kept calling your father when he wouldn't take your calls. You visited him as soon as he started talking to you again." And he'd done so much more, including letting Mr Winder live rent-free for two years in the house he'd bought when his father had lost his job.

"I could have tried harder to be close to him. *You* would have. You never give up on anyone."

Only on myself, she thought ironically.

"Don't think about it." She held him in her arms, caressing his hair. "Regrets are useless things, love. You can't change the past, only try to make the future better."

"I can't stop thinking about it." He held hard to her. "He's gone, and I can never tell him I'm sorry. It's just another regret in half a lifetime of them. I keep losing the people I love because I don't tell them the things I ought to."

For a long time she just let him shake, let the tears fall, let him hate himself. She heard him out, didn't attempt to soothe him with words that wouldn't help. She held him and kissed him over and over, her silence and her love the only balm she had.

When the shaking subsided, she knew the time had come.

"If you lose people you love through silence, we're two of a kind," she whispered, kissing his cheek. "I've been a coward too long, afraid of losing you, afraid of being hurt. I won't live my life in fear anymore. I'm sorry, this is probably the worst time to say it, but there may not *be* another time." She held his face in her hands again, looking deep into his eyes. "I am the most beautiful woman in the world to you, and you want me more than any other woman."

White-faced, dark rings beneath his eyes, he looked

strained, haggard with grief. But then slowly he smiled, the one that turned her insides to mush, and though the pain, the regret, was still there he looked like sunshine on the water, like a summer breeze through the trees: beautiful and whole. And the worst time somehow became the right time. "Yes."

"I haven't finished." She put a finger to his lips, smiling back. "You love me."

He smiled, looking puzzled. "Of course."

"No," she whispered, tinged with awe and joy. "You're in love with me."

He smiled again, his eyes coming to life as he understood: at last she believed in herself; she finally realised that a man as wonderful as Toby could be in love with her. "Of course."

He said it as if it was something she also should have known all along—and suddenly she realised she *would* always have known, if only she could have believed in herself the way she believed in him.

She touched his face the way he had touched hers minutes ago, her eyes shimmering with trust. "You are the most beautiful man in the world to me, and I want you so much I'm in pain. Tonight I'm going to make love to you all night, the man I love with all my heart."

"Are you certain, beloved?" he whispered against her mouth. "I'm your first kiss, your first love. If not for my selfishness, you'd—"

She held a finger to his mouth, smiling. "Did you need to taste every fruit in the world to be sure mangoes were always going to be your favourite?"

One side of his mouth quirked up. "No, but…"

"Did kissing or making love to any of those other women make you forget me, or want me less?"

The momentary cloud in his eyes at the mention of those women lifted at the strength and conviction in her voice. "They only made me want you more."

Her eyes lit; the finger at his mouth drew a slow, sensuous line along it. "Then accept the truth, Winder—I don't want to kiss anyone else." She kissed him, slow and deep. "I tried for years to get over you, but I only lied to myself. You're it—you're the only one. Love me, Toby."

One kiss, two, soft, slow and clinging…healing in words, without words. "I do. I always have, since the day you brought me home. I just didn't know how much until you collapsed and I faced the thought of life without you." After another, deeper kiss, he pulled back, his eyes searching hers. "I don't have protection, Giulia, and there's no way for us to get it without it hitting world news. You could fall pregnant."

A joy so poignant it was almost pain lit her entire body. Toby's child…

"I've dreamed of seeing you rounded with our child for years." He kissed her cheek, her throat. "But if you fall pregnant, beloved, I'll storm the damned palace to bring you home if I have to. I'll fight Charlie and Jazmine and the entire House of Hereditary Lords. I won't give you up, or our child, not to kings or princes or any national need."

Lost in the lovely dreams his declaration brought to life in her, she whispered, "Make me pregnant, Toby. Give me your child. Then Charlie would…"

Slowly, he looked up into her eyes, the fire dimmed. "Even when he's king, Charlie can't wave a magic wand to make me a duke or prince. He checked the law. He can't hand me Malascos like a gift. It has to be inherited at death, to a descendant." He shrugged. "I always knew I barely deserved you, even when you were my at-home girl. But you're not my Giulia now—you're the princess you were born to be. You belong in the palace. You deserve the adoration of everyone in Hellenia, and I don't have a place in that world."

How he could believe he didn't have a place, when he was a national hero, she didn't understand—or maybe she did.

She'd spent years not feeling pretty enough for him; he'd spent those same years feeling unworthy of her. The titles and castles only widened that gap in his mind.

"It isn't about adoration or fame or wealth to me," she said earnestly, staring into his eyes, pleading for him to understand. "If it were that, I'd walk away from it to be with you without looking back. You've seen what I do. It's so much more important than looking good, smiling, waving and having people love you."

"I do know—I understand, Giulia—but I am what I am. I'm a commoner, a simple fireman. Even if the Hellenican people would allow it, I can't ride on your wings or live in your shadow." He frowned and looked away from the devastation she knew was in her eyes. "I handled the intrusions, and everyone in my face and business in the palace, because it had a shelf life. Even all the knighthood stuff will pass. But even here, in my home country, I can't leave a hotel room to organise my father's funeral." He sighed. "I'll always love you, but I can't live my life surrounded by security, every hour planned, my most personal moments documented in the press, always giving some piece of me to fulfil the dreams and expectations of strangers."

Sadness swamped her as the last vestiges of her life's dream quietly splintered and fell to the ground; but she couldn't blame him. He'd sacrificed enough of his life to her health and happiness. It was time she gave him a priceless gift: his freedom, without chains of guilt. "It's all right," she whispered, trying not to cry.

"I won't ask you to stay with me," he whispered back. "No matter how much I need and love you."

Blackness swamped her eyes and heart as she saw the "Toby and Giulia" story dying right in front of her. "I couldn't forgive myself for choosing personal happiness over the welfare of a nation, and a royal family that's lost everyone else. I couldn't stand the regrets Yiayia and Papou suffered, or live in hiding."

As if he'd expected it, he nodded. He knew her so well.

"I'll always be the King's sister, the lost princess. There'll always be press interest in my life. You'd hate it, hate *me*, in the end."

"I could never hate you," he said quietly.

But you couldn't live my life either, even if we found a miracle. So I'm giving you the gift you deserve. She smiled at him. "We still have tonight."

He stood, lifting her in his arms, kissed her and carried her to the bed, lying her down on the cover. "What is it?" he whispered.

"Silly dreams," she whispered. "I always envisioned this as our wedding night." She bit her lip, embarrassed. "I've imagined my wedding since I was twelve. You were always the groom at the end of the aisle, the one I made my vows to."

His eyes darkened. "If your dream is silly, beloved, then so is mine." He pulled two boxes from his pocket, his face still and serious. "I've been carrying these around since the tenth anniversary of your release from the clinic. Wear them for me tonight."

He opened the first box: inside was a pretty ruby-and-diamond engagement ring. The second held matching wedding rings. "T-T…" She couldn't go on.

He pulled her rings from their boxes, his smile so tender it broke her heart. "Left hand, please."

She bit her lip as she held out her left hand. Looking into those summer-sky eyes so filled with love, finally she believed the heart of this magnificent, giving man was hers for life.

As he slid the rings on her finger, she stumbled through a clumsy vow, the words she'd relived in her mind a thousand times. "I promise to be true to you in good times and bad, and forsaking all others, love only you for all the days of my life."

As she slid the ring onto his wedding finger, he said, "There will never be another woman in my heart, Giulia. You are my wife, my love, now and for ever."

He kissed her, then walked to the bedroom door and closed it.

Hours later, Lia stood watching the fading lights of the city shimmering on the shifting waves of Sydney Harbour. Dawn was close.

She wore the satin robe the hotel had provided, her hair loose. She was barefoot, her body thoroughly loved, her mind and heart full. She'd hoped, believed, that if her first time was with Toby she could face the future with courage, and allow one of those suitable men the King favoured to give the country a backup heir or two.

Now, having loved the only man for her, she couldn't stand to think about another man's hands touching her. She was Toby's woman, heart, body and soul. She always had been. Now she always would be.

She wasn't surprised when his warm, muscled, firefighter's arms came round her. "Hey," she greeted him, snuggling back against his body.

"Hey," he said quietly.

He didn't ask the timeless question. He knew she was all right, that she had no regrets for the most poignant, beautiful night of her life. He waited for her to speak.

She couldn't tell him. He'd given up so much for her sake, for too many years. She had no doubt that, if she told him how she felt, he'd do it again. But this time he'd change jobs and countries, living alone for her sake, waiting for stolen moments with her, and his spirit would wither.

She kept looking out over the water, watching the soft fire of morning begin on the eastern side of Fort Dennison.

"God, how I wish I could ask you to stay, to marry me, my beautiful, beloved friend. I want you to stay with me in the house Papou built, have babies with me and live the life we both love."

"Don't, Toby, please don't." She closed her eyes. "It's a beautiful dream with no substance. You know it wouldn't happen, even if they let me go."

His voice was smoky-dark, husky with love. "Some people live their entire lives never knowing the kind of love we have. What we have comes only once in a lifetime."

A lifetime they couldn't have…

"Do you remember when I took your hand the day you came to live with us?"

He lifted her hair, kissing her neck. "Yes, of course."

"I walked home, so proud and happy. You were holding my hand, and it meant the world to me. I couldn't talk. I just kept thinking, 'I'm going to marry him,'" she said through a thick throat. "That's how long I've loved you."

His eyes were dark. "I've loved you from the same day. You pulled off a miracle for me, gave me a life and family, and I've adored you ever since."

Breathe, Lia. Remember to breathe. She concentrated on it until she had a measure of control. "I'll organise for you to meet your family today."

"It's done. The security contingent just needed a day to work out the logistics."

"Would you like me to come with you?" she offered tentatively.

He kissed her hair. "Best not to. They'd just turn it into another story."

"All right."

He lifted her hand, the one wearing his rings. "They're not like any of your royal jewels."

"No, they're not." *They're modest and sweet, like our lives before. A simple expression of your love: the only thing I ever wanted.* "Can I keep them?"

"I bought them for you." He pulled the wedding ring from her finger. "Look inside."

She read the inscription: Giulia, for ever.

Moved by unbearable sweetness, she turned in his arms. "I said 'I love you' so many times as we made love, you must be tired of hearing it, but I held it in so long. I love you so much."

"I'll never tire of hearing it, or knowing it." He kissed her with lingering sweetness. "Call me in the middle of the night if you need to. I'll always want to hear it. And if you need to hear how much I love you, I'll always say it back and mean every word."

He didn't say the rest: *when I'm here and you're gone.*

She blocked it from her mind. Her hands slipped beneath his robe to his waist, caressing it. They slid up to his chest and then his shoulders…and as the lovely thudding of desire took over again she whispered, "I need you," as she'd already said so many times on this, the only night they could have.

With a tender smile, he led her back to the bed.

Toby awoke with Giulia in his arms.

The morning sun flooded through the plate window, flickering over her golden skin; the reflections from the windows glistened on the hair spread over his pillows. She was deeply asleep, but her arm held him close, one of her legs tossed over his. Her lips moved over his chest as she breathed in and out.

So this was his dream come true; this was making *love.* He'd waited a lifetime for this night, this morning, and again she'd made it worth every moment. With every touch, every movement inside her, she'd unleashed a torrent of love on him like a burst dam: *I love you, I adore you, Toby. You're everything to me.* She had to have be in pain after the first time, yet she turned to him over and over in the night, loving his body with such utter reverence and pure love it had brought a physical ache to his chest.

And as she'd fallen into an exhausted sleep an hour ago, she'd whispered, "This is the only wedding night I'll ever have."

How she could love him so much when he'd screwed it up with her so many times through the years, he didn't know. All he knew was that she was the love of this lifetime or any other, and giving her up now would kill him. He'd fight the world to keep her here with him for life.

But there was no choice, nothing to fight. He could make her stay, but it would destroy her giving heart, her principles and her conscience. The woman he loved could never walk away from a promise and live with herself...

Surely there had to be a way? They were so *close* to it, so close he felt as if he was constantly groping towards a solution he just couldn't see. Love this perfect couldn't be for nothing.

A slight sound, a movement, made him look round. Charlie stood in the half-open doorway, looking at them.

Toby met his oldest friend's look of agonised indecision— deep, awkward sympathy and unspoken accusation—head on without apology.

As if feeling the disturbance, Giulia stirred, nuzzling his chest with her mouth. "I love you," she mumbled.

Charlie flinched, turned on his heel and walked away.

CHAPTER TEN

TOBY returned to the bed, where she lay sleeping over an hour later. He watched her for a moment, then bent and kissed her. "Giulia."

She stirred, stretched and smiled at him. "Toby." The name was a caress. She reached for him.

Her lovely dancer's body, golden and glowing and *loved* showed through the sheet, and he ached to love her again. "I've just come back from talking to Charlie. He wants to see you."

She must have seen something in his face; her arms dropped and her smile faded. "He came in here?" He nodded, and her mouth quirked. "Well, he always was on the overprotective side. So, is it the future king or the brother who wants to see me? Will it be pistols at dawn, or is he hounding you out of town?"

He held out his arms, knowing she was trying to hide her upset. She snuggled in, belonging there so naturally he wondered how he'd cope with the emptiness when she was gone. "He's distraught, Giulia. He'd hoped you and Max…"

Her voice was flat, hard. "These Marandis men seem to think they can order women to love where it's convenient for the nation."

"We knew he couldn't do anything," he said softly. "It's the way we were all raised. He has to put Hellenia first, just as you do. It's not his fault."

"I know," she said, and sighed. "But I can't do it, Toby, not even for the good of the nation. I thought making love to you would make it easier, but…" She shuddered against him.

Rage flooded him at the thought of any other man touching her, but he had to control it for her sake. "Don't think about it." Heaven knew he couldn't bear to. "He's agreed to look the other way with us until after the funeral."

"Oh." Giulia looked up at him, her eyes glowing dark with such joy it blocked his throat. "We have two more days?"

He nodded, but didn't add that Charlie had told him the King expected her to "get him out of her system" in that time. Why destroy the brief time they had?

She searched his eyes, sensed his disquiet. "Don't worry about what I said. According to the law as it stands, only the reigning king can force me to marry, and Charlie won't go that far."

Grimly, Toby wondered if that was true. This morning he'd seen a new Charlie, a man at war with himself, man against king. He'd never doubt how much Charlie loved his sister, but every decision must feel like Russian roulette to him. Which did he put first: family or the welfare of eight-million people? In royalty or government, collateral damage wasn't an excuse, it was a reason, a means to peace.

Was it overprotecting her to say nothing? If so, that was who *he* was: loving her, shielding her from this kind of pain was just what he did.

He just hoped Charlie didn't let her down when he was gone.

"Charlie can wait a bit longer," he said huskily, and bent to kiss her.

Two days later

"Thank God that's over." Charlie sighed and leaned back in the leather seating of the consulate limo.

The funeral had been a media circus, the wake just as bad. The press had tried to push past stony-faced ASIO, yelling questions at them all, but particularly at Lia and Toby about their relationship. Young girls had screamed Charlie's name as if he was a rock star. Politicians had angled for invitations; they'd all met the Prime Minister and state premier this morning, and had received regrets that they couldn't attend— as if it was the social event of the season instead of the funeral of an unemployed boiler-maker. Everyone inside had been searched for cameras, even phones had been confiscated.

It wouldn't stop some of them selling stories later:

What the Crown Prince Said To Me.

What The Princess Wore. How She Held Toby's Hand All Day.

How The Knighthood Has Changed Toby.

Lia said nothing in reply to Charlie's awkward comment. Toby said nothing either. She could feel the conflict inside him, the regret and grief—

"You okay, Grizz?" Charlie asked gruffly.

Something inside Lia became gentle, seeing her brother trying so hard to keep the friendship he'd always had. In the life they'd adopted, true friends were a luxury item, but friends who'd known them from childhood they trusted—there was only one.

Toby shrugged and looked out the window as they headed for the hotel, which was also surrounded by ASIO agents. "When do you all leave?"

Charlie looked stricken. "You're not coming? Not even to the coronation?"

When Toby didn't answer, Lia spoke. "We discussed it last night." *In bed,* she thought but didn't say. "It's best if he stays here for good."

She couldn't ask him to sacrifice his life for her any more. She loved him too much to make a kept man of him.

"It won't be the same without you, Grizz. You've been to every major event in my life." Charlie's voice was choked with emotion. "You're my brother."

Toby turned and looked at him for a long moment, but said nothing. There was no accusation in his expression, no anger, just…nothing.

"None of us can have everything we want, Charlie." Lia heard her voice shaking; she couldn't go on.

They pulled up at the kind of hotel they couldn't have dreamed of affording only six months before. Toby opened the door before the porter could. "I wish you all the best, Charlie, Jazmine. I'll send a gift. I'm going to pack." He looked at them all for a moment, eyes resting on Lia: *Come to me.* "Please thank the King for the funeral arrangements and help. It's time I returned to my own life."

He was inside the hotel moments later.

Charlie was pale, his eyes blank. "I—I never thought he could walk out on us like that, just leave us behind when we need him."

"He's not," Lia choked. "We walked out on him, and never looked back until we needed him. We've expected him to bend for us, cross the world for us, give up his life and career for us when we needed him, to be whatever we want when we want it. He came to Hellenia on request and left on cue. He put up with danger and humiliation, and rid Hellenia of its greatest threat. He's even been told by his *brother* that he's not good enough for the woman he loves, the woman whose life he saved, so don't talk about *him* walking out on us!"

Charlie whitened, swore and scrambled from the limo. "I have to make this right." He entered the hotel, wearing the personality of his future like a cloak from the moment he left the car. He smiled and waved to the press, spoke briefly to the security staff, and the hotel people eager to speak to a future king—but he was still at the lift within three minutes.

"They'll be fine," Jazmine murmured as the two women followed his lead, smiling and waving as they walked past the flashing cameras, heading for the special elevator reserved for the royal suites.

"I know." Lia knew it would be smoothed over between the two men. But things couldn't be as they had been in the past, not for any of them.

Even if he could find a way to become high enough for her, Toby couldn't stand the life she'd chosen. She couldn't refuse the privilege and duty that was her birthright, couldn't let any more of her people die because of her family's choosing love over duty. But the love of her lifetime was over after three days, she'd lost her lover and her best friend, and she had to learn to live without him.

When the elevator reached the suites, Lia said quietly, "I think it's also time I returned to my life. Excuse me, Jazmine."

"We'll come with you," Jazmine said, laying a hand on her arm.

Unable to stand being touched, Lia moved away. "If you don't mind, I'd rather go alone. I'll see you at—at the palace." She couldn't call Hellenia "home." Home was wherever Toby was.

Stop it. This could only ever have ended one way from the day I accepted the role of princess.

She walked into Toby's suite. Charlie's hand was on Toby's shoulder. He was pleading with his friend to understand, to come to his coronation. Toby was shaking his head, saying as little as possible.

She closed the door, filled with sadness. The day of "the Three Musketeers" was done. "Charlie, can you please leave us alone?"

"Lia, you've had three days with him without my interference," Charlie said quietly, his hand falling from Toby.

"And it's all we'll ever have," she replied, just as quiet.

"You get a lifetime with the woman you love, so please don't lecture me. Just leave."

White faced, her brother left without another word.

When he was gone, Toby kept packing a bag. She whispered, "Toby, look at me. *Please.*"

He looked worse than she'd ever seen him, grey and haggard with loss and grief. "So this is it?"

Unable to speak, she nodded.

"Ask me to go with you." His eyes burned dry and hard. "Just ask me, Giulia."

Tears spilled from her lashes. "I can't." *I love you too much.* She walked into his arms, holding him close. There couldn't be a worse possible day for this farewell, but it was all they had. "I'll miss you."

"Like the other half of me is missing," he agreed, mirroring her own words and hold from the first day he'd arrived in Hellenia.

The first day he'd kissed her.

"Promise me you'll eat well, look after yourself, and that you'll call me any time you need me."

Her heart cracked open. "I will, I promise. I have to go," she whispered, and broke away from him, bolting for the door.

Amid a multitude of flashing cameras, she returned to the limousine ten minutes later, head high, eyes bright and dry. She smiled and waved for the cameras. Her bodyguards walked each side of her; the jet was ordered and waiting. At the airport, her security detail surrounded her. Her personal assistant sat inside, awaiting orders. In a life of glittering beauty and fortune most would envy, Giulia Maria Helena Costa Marandis, Princess of Hellenia, felt only lost. Empty.

"She did the only thing she could, mate," Charlie said awkwardly. "I know—"

"No, you don't." Toby kept packing his bags. "You don't

know her. I didn't know her until recently. She'll do what you want, you can rely on her sense of duty. You won't have to worry about the anorexia either. She's too strong a woman to ever go back there. But if you make her marry and produce royal heirs before she's ready, you'll never have your sister again. You'll only have the princess."

Unable to deny it, Charlie paled. They'd all seen her complete withdrawal from the King. She'd been gracious and cold, and she'd been polite and remote with Charlie and Jazmine for the past few days. "What the hell do I do, Grizz? You tell me. I've bent over backwards to try to make it happen for you both!"

"He has, Toby," Jazmine said, her voice clogged. "We love you both. We want you to be happy. But how do we live with the consequences?"

"You don't. The people of Hellenia don't. Giulia and I have to," he stated flatly, knowing it wasn't fair, but he was way past caring. "We know you can't fix it, but we can't give you absolution or act as if it doesn't matter. There's a price for all of us." He flicked a glance at his oldest friend, seeing the unalterable pain there, but couldn't make himself feel it. "You avoid war. Take comfort in that."

"There'll always be a place for you in Hellenia, Grizz. A place with us. You're family." Charlie's voice was choked too. "Please, Grizz. Don't walk out on us."

"I wish I could do it," he said flatly. "I wish I was noble enough to give you all unconditional love. But I can't watch you marry her off to another man. I'd kill him. I'd kill anyone who touched her. The only way to avoid it is to be half a world away." He closed his bag and zipped it. "I have to go."

"Don't go, Grizz. Please, mate. Don't end our friendship like this."

"There's no way to avoid it." He picked up the phone and got reception. "This is Toby Winder in the Premier Suite. Has the cab arrived?"

When he hung up the phone, Charlie put a hand on his shoulder. "At least take the damn limo, Grizz. We don't need it until tomorrow."

Toby gently pulled away. "The limos and jets were only ever on borrowed time for me. Title or not, it's time I was myself again." After a moment, he asked, "What do you want to do about the house? It's in all our names."

"Keep it." Charlie stalked over to the window. Even from the distance, Toby could see his throat working. "Papou would want you to have it."

He nodded. "Thank you for all the years of friendship, Rip." He smiled at Jazmine, who was openly crying. "I wish you both all the best in life, lots of kids and a peaceful rule. I hope the coronation goes well."

He picked up his bags and walked out of the room.

CHAPTER ELEVEN

Six weeks later

"YOU DID SO WELL IN The Hague, my dear." The King smiled at her over the dining table. "Your speech to the European Court on the rights of women here has made the Lords aware of how the world will view us. They're ready to make further changes."

Lia said quietly, "I'm glad."

"You look so tired, Lia." He'd taken to calling her Lia since he'd seen her flinch at the formal name—Toby's name for her. "Perhaps you should take time off."

"Thank you, but no." She ate another mouthful of vegetables, wishing she could taste them. "I have a full schedule for the next three months, and I can't afford to reschedule anyone."

"Lia, Grandfather's right, you look exhausted and pale. You look totally stressed out." Charlie frowned, searching her face. "When's the last time you were out in the fresh air? I haven't seen you walk or run in a long time."

She felt the deadness touch her soul. "Charlie." The word wasn't a plea, it was a command to stop.

He ignored her. "You don't read or dance, either. And you don't cook. You love to dance and cook, Lia. Why don't you—?"

The lump filled her throat, a pain she couldn't swallow. Walking, running, reading or dancing—it was all Toby. Everything was Toby…

Desperate to avoid the inquisition, she shoved the chair back. "Excuse me." She was gone before anyone could speak, but she felt four worried sets of eyes follow her out of the room.

And she knew four hearts worried about her as she paced her room that night, walking until her mind finally shut down and she fell to the bed in a dreamless slumber. Three hours until the alarm went off and she started the rounds of life again.

The Coronation of King Kyriacos and Queen Jazmine of Hellenia

The Archbishop of Orakidis stepped back with a smile, throwing out his arm. "I present to you, King Kyriacos and Queen Jazmine of the Kingdom of Hellenia."

Looking serious and regal, Charlie and Jazmine stepped forward, resplendent in their scarlet-and-purple robes. The traditional crown of Hellenia rested on Charlie's head; the newly made matching crown that had replaced the traditional queen's tiara looked large and too heavy for Jazmine's small frame.

They must be blinded from all the flashes popping…

Lia watched from the marble balcony in the tiers above the dais beside the King—former king—who could no longer stand. As the third in line to the throne, she was expected to lead the way. She rose to her feet and bowed her head in traditional submission, then she smiled and began the applause.

Theo Angelis followed, smiling up at her in loving encouragement.

He'd been that way since she'd returned from Sydney. He'd handed all reins of power to Charlie and Jazmine, and refrained from asking the hard questions. It was no longer his place, he'd told her. He hadn't even complained when Charlie had said the coronation had to be put back four weeks out of respect for Toby's father's death.

Theo Angelis had also said nothing when Max had taken matters from everyone's hands the day after she'd walked out of the dining hall, making a public announcement that there wouldn't be a second royal wedding that included him.

Lia didn't understand Theo Angelis's silence; she was just grateful she didn't have the daily inquisition to face any more. Just getting through each day was challenge enough.

Charlie and Jazmine walked around the dais, then down the aisle of the cathedral, smiling and greeting every special guest by name.

Then, in the tenth row, the last row reserved for members of the nobility, a big bear of a man in a knight's cape with dark-and-golden, half-curling hair got to his feet to join the applause…

She swayed where she stood. The warmth and probably the colour drained from her face. Her hands fell to the rail and gripped hard. And she stared in shock and pain hunger and love.

He turned to look up at the balcony and smiled—but for the first time she felt no rush of joy, no gladness. Why, *why,* had Charlie made him come?

How was she going to face a state dinner with a thousand important guests, knowing he was there?

Toby saw her face, so stark and pale, so lovely, the dark hunger and pain too deep even to think of hiding it for the observers and cameras as she stared at him. He knew Charlie was right: he'd had to come today. She needed him…

So why hadn't she called him? He'd sent her text messages and emails, aiming for the old friendliness, but last week she'd sent her first message back: *please stop. I can't do this.*

By the time they were all seated at the state dinner that night and she hadn't come anywhere near him, not even to greet him, he realised he'd made it worse for her by being here. She wasn't the anorexic girl he could cajole into laughter and eating; she wasn't the homebody who lit up with the prospect of a bushwalk or cooking something. She was a woman strong enough to stand alone—but she was in love, in pain, and he couldn't save her from that. He wasn't her hero; he was the man who loved her. The man who'd left her alone in an alien world.

He'd left her as alone as she'd been when he'd gone on those dates, leaving her to imagine the worst. He'd walked out of her life because he couldn't be her supplicant, her hidden lover, couldn't stand to be in second place with her.

She needs your friendship to live.

She'll always have it.

Would he never stop letting her down because of his stupid fears and foolish pride, never feeling good enough?

He came to her room at two in the morning, when she'd finally finished settling all the visiting dignitaries and had made them feel suitably important. Though the room was dark, she wasn't in bed. She was in jeans and a pullover, barefoot and pacing the room. "I knew you'd come," was all she said. She didn't look at him.

He looked at the tiara tossed on the bed, the shoes obviously kicked off and left to fall, the ten-thousand-dollar dress half-lying on the floor. His scrupulously neat Giulia hadn't even let the maid in the room to tidy it.

The rings he'd given her were on her right hand now. The clothes she wore were bargain-bin stuff from a Sydney store, from her old life. Her eyes had dark hollows beneath them, and she was far too pale.

"Do you want me to go?" She was too on edge for this.

"Yes," she snapped. "No!" she cried when he turned to go, and when he turned back she was there in his arms. He held her close, breathing in her simple lavender scent with a sense of coming home.

"I *miss* you," she rasped, holding him so hard his chest hurt. "I don't feel *alive.*"

"I know, love, I know." He'd given his life to her so long ago that without her, even with his privacy and his job and all the things he claimed he needed, he'd just existed, stumbling through each day; he hadn't lived. She wasn't there. She wasn't there, and everything he'd wanted in his life was dust and ashes.

"Charlie says he ordered books for you that you didn't read, arranged a day out in the mountains you didn't take," he said softly, kissing her hair.

"I can't. I can't do those things any more. They're all you. They're you and me, and I can't bear to."

He tipped up her face and kissed her with all the aching tenderness in his heart. He didn't speak. What could he say to that?

"I was—I thought I was—but then you came, and the pain started all over again." She shook her head against his shoulder. "Please, just go home."

If there was one thing he knew now, it was that they couldn't live apart. "Ask me to stay, my Giulia," he whispered. "Ask me to make love to you, to be here day and night for you for the rest of our lives."

"Don't you understand? I couldn't stand it when I'm only going to lose you again!" She broke away fiercely. "I can't keep going through this. I cried all night when I got my period. I— It was a week late, and I'd hoped…"

And she'd done that alone, too, and survived. So much strength and courage.

"Then ask me to stay because I need you," he said quietly. "I'll stay for ever, beloved. I'll be whatever you need me to be."

She shuddered. "Don't, Toby. I couldn't do that to you!"

A tiny bud of anger began to blossom in his heart at her constant denials. "What if I said I want to stay—that I *need* to stay—to be with you?"

"You don't. You're doing this for me, I know you are." She was hugging herself, arms around her waist in self-comfort. "I can't let you sacrifice anything more for my sake. Please, just go!"

He stared at her, wondering when in the past six weeks she'd forgotten all the words he'd said as they'd made love. "Loving you is no sacrifice, Giulia. It never has been. You're the love of my life. We can compromise. Losing the love we have is the sacrifice neither of us needs to make!"

"You'd hate me in the end. I saw your face when you asked the family if you could live with us. You hated being put in a beggar's position." She wouldn't turn back, wouldn't look at him. "It's what you'd always have to be with me. No matter how much I need and love you, it wouldn't be enough."

Adrenaline surged through him. Fighting for his love or a fire, it made his pulse pound and his limbs itch with the urge to *do*. He grabbed her shoulders and turned her to face him. "That's not true. Just having you love me is more than enough, more than I could dream of having. Giulia, don't you see?" he growled. Frustration filled him when she shook her head again. He hated hearing his own words given back to him with such faith. Damn it, she knew him inside and out; why had she believed him when he'd said he needed freedom and privacy more than he needed her? He'd barely believed it himself. He'd lied to them both for the sake of his pride and to set her free to do what she must, and now they were both paying the price for it.

"Asking for my family was the best thing that ever happened to me, Giulia. It gave me a life I love, with people I belong to, belong with. I know that now, because everything I said I wanted is empty without you." He looked in her hurting dark eyes, hoping like hell she'd understand. "Asking for what you need doesn't make you low, it makes you human. I'm asking, Giulia. I need to stay. I need *you.*"

"Not like this. I know you, Toby." She smiled at him through lonely tears. She stood in a shaft of cold moonlight, small and fragile, yet too strong to let him in. "Go home. I need you to be happy."

"I can't be happy without you," he rasped, bending to kiss her. God help him, he needed her like air, like sunlight, and she was leaving him in blackness.

A cloud obscured the moon; darkness fell over her as she turned from him. She shook her head as he reached for her. "Please go."

At that, the fury of her self-image flooded him heart and soul. After all these years, she still couldn't see how much he needed her. He was furious at himself, because she was only holding to the words he'd told her, but even more so at her because she was trying to give him what she thought he needed, but still didn't know that life without her—best friend, lover and yes, damn it, even princess—wasn't *life.*

So he'd prove to her he was nobody's supplicant. And he'd prove that, while she might be able to live without him, she damn well wasn't going to get the chance to try. He wouldn't let her!

He scooped her up in his arms, his mouth on hers in a deep, drowning kiss until she was shivering against him and helplessly kissing him back, her hands caressing his skin with feverish hunger. "Now tell me to go," he snarled.

Great, fawn eyes stared up at him, aching with love. Trembling hands pulled him down to her for another kiss. "I can't," she whispered. "I need you, Toby, I need you."

"Good." He smiled grimly as he carried her to the bed.

Charlie summoned him to the royal study soon after dawn, and his personal assistant actually laughed as he delivered the message over the phone. "King Kyriacos requests your immediate presence in his study. He said to tell you it's either an emergency or a miracle delivered via a lawyer. I'm waiting outside Princess Giulia's door for you."

Arrested by the words, by the palace officer's acceptance of his relationship with Giulia, Toby flung off the covers to dress. "I'll be back," he whispered when she stirred, reaching for him in her sleep.

She smiled and drifted back into much-needed rest.

Charlie's assistant ushered Toby through the quiet palace and into the sitting room that used to be King Angelis's. It looked like Charlie's room now, with the gilt-laden furniture taken out and replaced by half the amount, all strong, clean, masculine pieces. "What was worth waking me up for after about an hour's sleep? If this is about my staying with Giulia—"

"It isn't. I knew you would." Charlie wasn't even looking at him; he was sitting behind his desk, staring down at a sheaf of papers with a stunned look on his face.

"What's going on, Rip?" he asked, sensing something strange was going on. "What's that you're reading? I gather it's something to do with me?"

"Yes, it is," Charlie muttered. "The King told me a little secret you saw fit to tell him but not me." Hellenia's new king held up a thick file filled with packets and what looked like letters. "These are from Papou, through his *other* lawyer."

Beginning to understand, Toby sat down. "So this stuff is from Mr Mendoza?"

"Yes—the lawyer with whom he drew up his *real* will, just before he died, with specific instructions," Charlie said slowly. "The lawyer you always knew about, if the letter that came with Papou's will is any indication."

Slowly, he nodded. "I'm sorry, Rip. Yiayia and Papou made me promise to keep it a complete secret."

"Yes, I understand—but, damn it, knowing this could have

saved us all some heartburn." Charlie shrugged, face grim. "By Papou's arrangements, this lot should have reached me before the wedding, but Mr Mendoza passed away just before that, and the new lawyer only found them in the safe after we got ASIO onto the job."

Toby frowned. "I gather this new will has some legacy or instructions for me?"

"It's got a whole lot more than that, you idiot." Charlie flung a set of papers his way. "This changes *everything*."

"The King said it changed nothing," Toby argued, his heart pounding.

"Well, of course he would, wouldn't he? But if you'd told me the truth about what happened fifteen years ago we wouldn't be in this mess now!"

CHAPTER TWELVE

TOBY was gone when she woke up, with not even the traditional note on the pillow. Not knowing what happened, she got up, showered and dressed. She had a lot of duties to attend to this morning, with all the guests.

Except it was lunch time. She'd slept for seven hours?

She bit her lip and grinned, thinking of her own proven insomnia-remedy.

Ask me to stay because I need you. He'd proven through the night, loving her with a desperation and power that had showed her he'd missed her as much as she'd missed him, that his love for her was as timeless and unending as hers for him.

Ask me to stay, my Giulia.

Dared she do just that? Could she believe she was enough for a lifetime, when she could only give him what they had now—a beautiful affair in the shadows?

She headed down the stairs to find him, but Charlie caught up with her before she made the stairs. "It's so good to see you smiling again, Lia."

She hugged her brother. "Thanks for bringing him to me," she whispered.

Charlie reddened and grinned. "What? I had to have all the nobles together for coronation, and he's one now whether he likes it or not."

She smiled again, but it soon faded. "What happens if I'm pregnant?"

To her surprise, Charlie, the most old-fashioned brother in the world, shrugged. "We'll deal with it if it happens. You won't be the first unmarried pregnant princess—maybe the second."

Lia blinked. "Is this the same brother who barrelled me out for daring to even think I could love a commoner?"

"Yeah, actually, it is—the same brother who always loses his temper and speaks without thinking it through. I'm pretty new at this royalty caper, and I won't always get it right." He grinned at her expression. "What, did you think I'd disown you?"

She smiled back. "Well, at least get me married to some suitable noble at gunpoint before I started showing."

"Maybe I deserve that," he said ruefully. "But none of us want you to be as unhappy as you've been the past weeks, Lia. Trust me, okay?"

She looked at her brother, saw his eyes shining with new-found strength.

"Jazmine and I know what's going on in our country, and in our family. We're doing what we can to make you and the people happy."

"Do you know where Toby is?" she asked, to test that trust. Would he answer?

Charlie nodded. "You'll see him later. I needed him to go to Malascos for me. He'll be back by this afternoon." He hesitated. "I need you to clear your schedule today. I've called an extraordinary meeting of the Hereditary House of Lords. We have another shock to deliver to the crusty diehards in parliament—" he grinned "—and we need you to be there. For backup, you know?"

She frowned, trying to think. "I'm supposed to meet a representative of the European Court about the conditions for women here, to follow up on—"

"Reschedule it," Charlie interrupted her, his tone commanding. "We need you there."

She peered at him. "What's going on, Charlie? I need to have some information ahead of time if I'm to help you."

Obviously relieved she was obeying without further argument, he kissed her cheek. "I think it's best if you look as shocked as everyone else. It'll work better."

"All right," she said slowly. How to say it? "Charlie, Toby said he wants to stay…with me."

Charlie sighed. "Look, Lia, today's meeting's important, okay? We'll get to your problems soon. I've only been king eighteen hours, and maybe I don't have any rabbits to pull out of hats for you just yet."

Ashamed, she nodded. "I'll call the European Court representative and reschedule."

Extraordinary meeting of the Hereditary House of Lords

Lia sat beside Jazmine as Charlie stood up in the royal box. He was ready to make his first announcement as the King of Hellenia. Lia whispered to her sister-in-law, "What's going on?"

Jazmine grinned. "Stop cheating, Lia, and wait like everyone else." Her brows lifted. "We're about to throw a firecracker right into the dry old powder."

Lia smiled, but couldn't help wondering if Toby was back. She had to tell him…

Tell him what? Stay for my sake, make me happy at your own expense?

Loving you is no sacrifice, Giulia, he'd said…

"The Queen and I called this meeting because we have several questions needing resolution." Charlie's voice broke into her thoughts. He was standing tall over all the seated lords. "First and foremost, there is the pressing question you all wish answered—that of the marriage of my sister, Princess Giulia, to a suitable consort."

Lia stiffened in her seat. She glared at Charlie, who pretended not to see it. Jazmine wouldn't look at her either.

"I know you all have your opinions as to whom she should marry."

Pandemonium broke out as all the lords yelled their opinion, or tossed a name in the ring, as if she was a lucky-door prize, she thought disgustedly. This was why Charlie wanted her here?

"She can only marry a Hereditary Lord, one of his sons, or a prince!" one of the counts with a marriageable son yelled.

"That's true," Charlie agreed calmly. "Now please bear with me, I'm not trying to go against the laws. I brought this up because the Queen and I are aware of the rumours regarding my sister and my oldest friend, Sir Toby Winder, while he was here in Hellenia. I wish to resolve this. You all know him, or know of him—he did so much for our nation in the four months he was here, including risking his life to save others. During our last meeting, he was knighted for the rescue of the Grand Duke of Falcandis, and for uncovering the plot by Lord Orakis to destroy all the healing we've worked so hard to achieve."

What was Charlie trying to achieve with this line of argument?

"Yes, and we agreed with it—but a commoner can go no higher than a knight." That same count was red-faced with the force of his voice. "He cannot receive a hereditary title worthy of asking for the hand of the Princess Royal!"

The lords all nodded, some shouting, and Lia's pounding heart slowed and sank. Why had Charlie brought her here, to break her heart over again? How he brought Toby back to Hellenia only for her to lose him, to say another unbearable goodbye?

"Again, that's accepted." Charlie kept his cool. "A commoner cannot gain a higher title than knight, and cannot ask for the hand of my sister. Since Princess Giulia and the Grand Duke of Falcandis have refused to wed, the question of her marriage remains open for the moment."

At the decision in his voice, the lords' din died down.

"Moving on, there is one thing that confuses me still about the laws regarding inheritance and adoption."

The lords sat forward, interest in every face. They seemed to thrive on debate.

"May an adopted son inherit lands and titles, along with any true children a hereditary lord or duke might have?" Charlie asked, his tone carrying no more than mild query.

To Lia's surprise, it was Theo Angelis who spoke up, sitting at the back of the royal box. "If the child is legally adopted by the laws of the nation before he or she reaches their majority, and accepts the name of the family, then he or she is entitled to whatever the lord leaves in his will to that child."

"Ah, thank you, Your Majesty," Charlie said, giving Theo Angelis the title for life he deserved. "And that is Hellenican law? We are all agreed?"

The lords all nodded.

"Then, in light of your agreement, I want to share with you some papers pertaining to my grandfather, the former Grand Duke of Malascos, which only came to my attention this morning. This includes a set of full and legal adoption papers for his adopted son."

The House broke into a hubbub of sound. Lia, hardly daring to hope this was real, swung her gaze to Jazmine, who grinned at her and winked before she walked to her husband's side.

She looked at Theo Angelis. He sat stiff on his throne, staring only at Charlie, but there was something in his eyes; he knew what was going on.

Charlie smiled at the assembled room, waiting until the

sound died down again. "I'd always known my grandfather called Sir Toby his adopted son—but I thought it a courtesy title. I never knew my grandparents had made it formal and legal. But here is the irrefutable proof, stamped by the Australian government. Fifteen years ago, my grandparents, Kyriacos Charles Marandis and Giulia Maria Marandis, adopted Tobias Andrew Winder while he was still a minor according to law. They changed his name to Tobias Andrew Winder Marandis, with all the privileges and responsibilities that go with the name."

And she'd thought the sound before was pandemonium? Now the shouting sounded like a bunch of football hooligans attacking the winning team.

Charlie gave them a minute or two, then spoke right over them, his voice strong and implacable. "My grandparents also made a will, leaving everything to the three of us equally. After Princes Michael and Angelo died, leaving my wife the sole heiress to the throne of Hellenia, my grandfather obviously realised King Angelis would try to discover if his cousin had any male issue. He lodged a final will with the same lawyer that arranged Sir Toby's adoption. He stipulated that this will be released only if my grandfather's real identity should become known and the question of inheritance was raised." Charlie's smile grew. "There are too many clauses and codicils to read now, such as which titles and lands my friend or I should have from my grandfather's many Hellenican possessions, so I will now read you the pertinent part of my grandfather's real last will and testament."

In a slow, deep voice, he read, "'In the event that my grandson Kyriacos Charles Costa Marandis should inherit the title of Crown Prince of Hellenia, then to my adopted son, Tobias Andrew Winder Marandis, I bequeath my Grand Duchy of Malascos, with all attendant rights and wealth.'"

Dead silence filled the House as Charlie finished speaking.

All eyes turned to the old king. When he neither moved nor spoke, their collective gazes swung back to the new King and the Queen now standing beside him.

The real transfer of power happened in that moment, the shift of allegiance from the old to the young, the past to the future.

Charlie drew Jazmine close. "The Queen and I therefore wish to introduce you to the fourteenth Hereditary Grand Duke of Malascos, His Grace Tobias Andrew Winder Marandis." His free hand swept to one of the alcoves reserved for the six Grand Dukes of the nation.

The door behind it opened, and Lia saw Toby, her beautiful Toby, walk forward, a resplendent stranger in the scarlet, purple and gold robes of Malascos, the cloak pinned with the royal eagle.

He looked at her and smiled.

Lia didn't know she'd jumped to her feet until her knees gave way. An aide shot out a hand to steady her.

In the alcove beside where Toby stood, a man got to his feet and clapped. "The Fourteenth Grand Duke!" he shouted.

Max. Of course it was Max…

The other four Grand Dukes stood and applauded, leading the way.

And then, in the stalls below, the lords began to cheer.

Last, but far from least, Theo Angelis nodded at Toby with a small smile before he joined in the applause: royal approval.

Oh, surely any moment that alarm would go off and she'd wake up…?

Jazmine pressed a handkerchief into Lia's hand. "Breathe, Lia," her sister-in-law whispered with a smile. "It's really happening."

Lia gasped in a breath and groped for Jazmine's hand, unable to speak.

When the applause finally quietened, Charlie lifted a hand.

"I have one more letter here, outlining my grandfather's final wishes for us, his beloved son and grandchildren. Most of it is private, so I'll skip to the important part: 'having seen the demise of the royal family in Hellenia during the past twenty years, I realised that you, my beloved adopted son and grandchildren, will be needed there. I have done my best to prepare you for your future tasks, by teaching you the language and culture, and instilling in you all a deep sense of duty and self-sacrifice—the kind I could never make. So, to my beloved granddaughter Giulia, I give my dearest love and my unwavering faith that you will be the best princess Hellenia could ask for. I have only one wish for you—to marry my adopted son, Tobias Andrew Winder Marandis.'"

He smiled over at her, mouthed, "How's this for a rabbit, sis?" and Lia had to mop more tears. "'To my adopted son, Tobias, I bestow upon you my blessing, my complete belief that you will be an exceptional Grand Duke and will work selflessly to help repair my shattered nation as you helped keep our family together in times of crisis. I humbly ask that you accept the position I forsook, and that you care for and love my granddaughter for the rest of your lives, as she will love and care for you. I believe you are the perfect man for the task ahead—and for my Giulia. To you all, my dearest love and hope for your understanding at the magnitude of the secret I kept from you.'"

By the time Charlie's voice came to a halt steeped in emotion, Lia was already on her feet, walking across the House. She heard no more, didn't know what the lords said, didn't care what Theo Angelis thought. Hardly aware of people milling around her, smiling or moving out of her way, or opening the small doors before her, she just kept walking as if in a dream. All she could see was Toby, giving her that wonderful, heart-melting "I love you" smile.

Finally, at last, she reached him and put her hand in his. "My Lord Duke," she whispered, and sank into a deep curtsey.

"It's Your Grace, actually." Eyes twinkling, he lifted her face with a finger and raised her to face him. "Your Royal Highness, you wish to speak to me?"

The question burst from her. "Did you know about the adoption and the change of name?"

He nodded. "Of course I knew. Yiayia and Papou told me about the Marandis name, but said there were reasons I had to keep the adoption and the Marandis name an absolute secret from everyone. I gave my word to keep it secret until Papou's letter released me and gave me a choice." He hesitated, and said, "I did tell the King, weeks ago. I hoped that being a Marandis by name might give me some right to marry you. At first he said it made no difference—my low-class bloodlines negated any adoption. But about a week ago he told Charlie, and had already begun digging for the truth." He smiled again. "All he said this morning was, 'make her happy again, Toby'."

"Oh…" She blinked back tears of joy. "So…is this why your parents really disowned you?"

He gave her a wry grin. "Even the twenty-five grand Papou paid each of them to sign the papers didn't make them forgive me for wanting to be a Costa…Marandis." He shrugged. "I always wondered how Papou could be so financially independent for a humble son of a bricklayer. Apparently he came into a fair few million at his majority, and he managed to take a million of it with him." He added softly, "You realise my family will expect us to share the wealth? They'll expect to visit, too, and become at least part-time members of the royal family. In short, becoming a Winder won't be easy."

She smiled, but didn't really care about his family's expectations or sharing the wealth at the moment. Her worried gaze searched his. "Are you sure you want to marry me, Toby? You said…"

He kissed the hand he held. "I said a lot of things, beloved, all of which came from a deep sense of unworthiness—to have joined your family in the first place, to be here at all—but mostly I felt unworthy of you, your love." He gave her that smile again, and she ached to kiss him. "I'll show you Papou's letter to me when we're alone. He was...most persuasive."

"You're certain of this?" Her eyes clung to his, begging for truth.

"I'm certain of only one thing at this point, my Giulia—that I can survive without you, but I don't *live.* I tried to return to my old life, but after a few weeks I knew it was hopeless. I need you with me, beloved. Wherever you are, I have to be. So if you're a princess, I'm a prince, if that's what it takes."

"But you'll be unhappy with all the attention."

"Perhaps I will be sometimes—but as I hope I've shown you the past ten years, you're worth any sacrifice, my beloved, beautiful Giulia. *Any* sacrifice. This kind of love comes only once to each man and woman," he added softly.

And finally, for the first time, she felt true joy inside her, a bubble of purest happiness bursting through her heart and body. It was real; she was loved by one man, wanted and loved for life. And it was her best friend, her lover, her Toby.

Her life's dream had come true.

Looking up at him with adoring eyes, she dipped into another curtsey. "Will you please accept my hand in marriage, my lord—um—Your Grace? Will you become what you've always been to me—my prince? Because you've always made me feel like a princess."

He kissed her hand again, pulling both rings from her right hand and slipping the modest ruby-and-diamond ring onto her left. "Giulia, for ever."

"Toby, for ever," she whispered, tears of brilliant, glittering happiness streaming down her face, aching with the need to kiss him. "Toby..."

"I know, beloved, I know. But not only did you have me to

yourself all last night, you embroiled me in this right royal scenario by bringing me home all those years ago. Now you must wait for kisses while I endure the tedious ritual of meeting all my fellow dukes and lords." He grinned at her. "I hope there are no further motions of historical importance for our perusal today?"

She bit her lip over laughter. "I certainly hope not. A few of 'em look ready to pass out with the shock as it is."

He winked. "Go and sit, beloved. This may take quite a while."

In a daze of happiness, Lia returned to her seat. She gave Jazmine and Charlie a blinding smile, and returned their hugs and kisses, whispering thanks.

She turned to Theo Angelis then, who gave her a tender smile. If he'd been outwitted by his cousin after death, he'd still worked for her happiness—and the tiny, almost invisible wink told her he was putting family above bloodline. He loved her.

"Your Highness, may I offer my congratulations at your royal engagement?"

At the head of a line of lords, Max stood, grinning at her, his arms open. Laughing, she hugged him; then she turned her attention to the next lord waiting to congratulate her, and the next. And all the while she kept her gaze on Toby as he met his new peers with the grace and poise Papou had so painstakingly taught him years ago, just as he'd taught him the Hellenican language.

Papou had planned this all along, had prepared them all not merely for royal life, but for the love of a lifetime. And Lia's heart whispered her thanks to a wise, loving old man who had always seen into their hearts.

EPILOGUE

Seven months later

"I CAN'T BELIEVE IT, look at how you've grown in a month! Hello, little one." Giulia was on her knees, talking to Jazmine's rounded stomach. "It's your Aunty Lia, who's going to teach you so many bad things."

Jazmine laughed and hugged Giulia, touching her stomach in turn. "Hello, littler one—it's your Aunt Jazmine, and your mama is telling awful fibs. She's always been a good girl, and she'll teach your cousin to dance as beautifully as she does." The ultrasound had shown that Charlie and Jazmine's first child was a girl.

From beside him on a brocaded settee—Toby saw Charlie and Jazmine hadn't simplified the entire palace as yet—Charlie grinned and thumped him on the shoulder. "So, congratulations, Dad-to-be. How does it feel?"

"When Giulia is the mother, it's perfect. Better than this prince caper, anyway," he added in haste when Charlie pretended to gag. "Behave yourself, Rip. None of that crass-fireman behaviour. Maintain some royal dignity, please."

The King of Hellenia laughed. "Yeah, right. I'll have to remember that line for the kids when they come. So how's life in Malascos?"

"Very much like life in Sydney in some ways, just on a grander scale." Before their wedding, which had come after Toby had gone through two months of intense social and physical training for the role, he and Giulia had made the decision to make the traditional Marandis home in the beautiful mountainous region of Malascos their own. They had chefs, maids and servants, but twice a week they gave everyone the night off. On those nights they cooked together, cleaned the kitchen, watched TV, danced together in the ballroom, or walked in the extensive gardens. Once a month they took turns flying their small jet to the Summer Palace to spend time with Charlie and Jazmine, and to take tea with Theo Angelis.

On their days off from royal duties they gave their security staff a scare with the mountains they climbed, or by riding their mountain bikes, but Toby figured the security staff needed something to worry about. Orakis was still on the run, Theo Angelis lived in quiet retirement in the northern wing of the Summer Palace with Puck by his side, and Charlie and Jazmine had brought a far more relaxed, happy rule to the country with an emphasis on bringing security and modern living to their people.

And day and night, he was with Giulia. It was all he could ask of life.

"You're both happy?" Charlie asked as he always did, with a trace of anxiety he'd probably never lose. Toby knew *he* wouldn't. He'd devoted his life to his wife's health and happiness for too many years to relax now, even though he knew that, of the two of them, she was the stronger. If he ever lost her...

To banish old shadows, he grinned and called to Giulia, "Wife?"

She turned, her laughing face softening with love. "Husband?"

To outsiders, the terms might seem bland, ordinary—but

they'd fought long and hard for the right to say them. Now they treasured the simple pronouns as others would jewels or money. They'd never take the beauty of their life together for granted.

"Charlie wants to know if we're happy."

"Does he, now?" Giulia ran to him, settled on his lap with a breathless laugh, and kissed him, slowly and lingering. Her fingers performed the tiny, almost invisible caresses on his neck that drove him crazy. "It's been five hours," she whispered in his ear. "That's at least an hour too long…"

"Insatiable woman," he whispered back, too soft for Charlie to hear. No matter how close they were, there were some things men didn't want to know. Charlie definitely wouldn't want to know his sister couldn't get enough of her husband.

"Hmm." She kissed his ear. "I've had the worst case of the hots for you for over fourteen years, Winder. Did you think a few puny months of constant love-making would get rid of it?"

"I certainly hope not, Mrs Winder. Nor in a few years. I fervently hope it lasts a lifetime."

Sometimes, in the middle of the night when she thought he was sleeping, she'd caress his body with feather-light, tender hands and lips. "My man at last," she always whispered, "My husband. I'm Lia Winder." The wonder in her voice made him ache to turn and kiss her every time—but it was her private moment, and, so long as she thought he didn't know, she kept doing it.

The wonder to him was that, in a life filled with riches, glamour and titles, his princess wife treasured the simple things the most: she treasured *him*.

She melted against him when he called her Mrs Winder, as he'd known she would. "Toby…"

The slow caress of her fingertips was making him shudder inside with hot need. "Soon, beloved. Now, behave yourself. I think we're grossing out your brother."

Charlie was red-faced, but his eyes were soft as he saw his

ister and best friend so happy. Jazmine was standing behind Charlie, massaging his shoulders, kissing his hair. "Newly-weds," she teased, laughing. "They just can't control them-selves."

"Says the old married woman, with five months' more ex-perience," Giulia mocked, smiling in turn as Charlie turned is face to kiss his wife's hand.

"Oh, sorry, I was looking for the bachelor's pad. Obviously 've wandered into Honeymoon Heaven, with *both* my ex-anceés. I'd better retreat to the nearest sports bar before the nvy kills me."

All four of them turned and grinned at Max. Charlie waved eir friend in. The four royals had made a small circle of inti-nate friends who knew their king, queen, prince and princess ad no desire for any formal bows or titles. "Hey, Max. How id it go?"

Max grinned, blew kisses at Giulia and Jazmine, and flung imself into a chair. "He left Majorca the day I arrived. I just nissed him on the Spanish mainland, too. At a best guess, I nink he's somewhere in Africa now."

Toby didn't have to guess who Max was speaking of. He'd nade it his personal mission to hunt down Orakis, leaving ight after the second royal wedding.

As the men talked politics, Jazmine motioned to Lia with er hand. Lia moved off Toby's lap, trailing her fingers over is shoulder as she left him. She couldn't be in a room with im, near him, without touching him somehow.

"I don't think Max was joking about the envy," Jazmine whispered. "I've been thinking…"

Lia laughed and hugged her sister-in-law. "Yiayia and Papou would have loved you. They were so happy together, hey were always trying to matchmake somebody they knew. They certainly made sure of Toby and me."

They turned towards Max, speculating on which lady they knew who could make him happy.

"Uh-oh," Charlie murmured. "Look at them, Grizz."

Toby looked at his wife and sister-in-law, both staring at Max with similar expressions. "Um, Max?" he rumbled. "You might want to discourage the women, and fast, before they find you fiancée number three."

Max was off his seat like a shot, and stalked over to the Queen and Princess with mock-sternness in his dark-blue eyes.

Toby chuckled. "I wonder who they have in mind for him. I'll have to pump Giulia for the info."

Charlie laughed. "Bet she doesn't tell you. Jazmine won't tell me for love or money. They wouldn't trust us not to tell him."

"You're probably right." He glanced at them again, at the sumptuous room around them. "Weird, isn't it, all this? About a year ago, we were single Aussie firemen."

"Crazy," Charlie agreed. "I still can't get used to it. Every day."

"Crazy, wonderful," he said, knowing what his friend meant. "How the hell did we ever get this lucky?"

Giulia came over to him at that moment. "Dobber," she mock-growled, using the irreverent Aussie term for a tittle tattle.

He grinned. "Promise to keep it to myself if you tell me who she is."

She shook her head and laughed, hugging him. "No way."

Charlie grinned and ambled over to Max and Jazmine, giving them a private moment.

Toby's brow lifted at her denial. "How can you expect my help in your matchmaking ventures if you don't confide in your long-suffering husband?"

"Who said I needed your help?" she retorted haughtily. "And, while you're surely long enough—" she grinned looking him up and down to emphasise his height "—you're not suffering *anything,* my Lord Prince."

"Listen to your mother, son," Toby murmured, caressing her belly—they'd just discovered they were having a boy. "Keeping secrets from me after all these years."

"What are you talking about? I *always* kept secrets from you."

He chuckled, bent her over his arm and kissed her. She loved those romantic gestures. "Such as how much you adore me…Mrs Winder."

Her eyes softened again as she whispered her love, and drew him back down for another kiss, ignoring the collective groans of their unwilling audience.

Toby didn't care what anyone said or what ribbing he received for being madly in love with his wife. Every minute with her, every kiss, still felt like a gift from God. Part of him still expected the alarm to go off, and that he'd be alone in his bed in Ryde, aching for Giulia and unable to speak, so completely unworthy of her.

Instead he awoke in a castle, of all places, with his adoring wife in his arms, a prince to her princess. Their first baby was on the way, and instead of facing fires he had a job he hadn't known would be as satisfying as it was exhausting when he'd taken it on. When life, the press or the job overwhelmed him, he retreated somewhere with Giulia and within moments she made the world bearable again. Far more than bearable, it was exquisite because she was there. She made every moment of his life rich, with a love so complete he had no room for self-doubt.

With Giulia by his side, he could be anyone, do anything.

We'll be spotlighting a different series every month throughout 2009 to celebrate our 60th anniversary.

Look for Harlequin® Presents in July!

TWO CROWNS, TWO ISLANDS, ONE LEGACY
A royal family, torn apart by pride and its lust for power, reunited by purity and passion

Step into the world of Karedes beginning this July with

BILLIONAIRE PRINCE, PREGNANT MISTRESS
by
Sandra Marton

Eight volumes to collect and treasure!

REQUEST YOUR FREE BOOKS!
2 FREE NOVELS PLUS 2
FREE GIFTS!

HARLEQUIN® Romance®

From the Heart, For the Heart

YES! Please send me 2 FREE Harlequin® Romance novels and my 2 FREE gifts (gifts are worth about $10). After receiving them, if I don't wish to receive any more books, I can return the shipping statement marked "cancel". If I don't cancel, I will receive 4 brand-new novels every month and be billed just $3.84 per book in the U.S. or $4.24 per book in Canada. That's a savings of at least 15% off the cover price! It's quite a bargain! Shipping and handling is just 50¢ per book.* I understand that accepting the 2 free books and gifts places me under no obligation to buy anything. I can always return a shipment and cancel at any time. Even if I never buy another book, the two free books and gifts are mine to keep forever.

114 HDN EYU3 314 HDN EYKG

Name	(PLEASE PRINT)	
Address		Apt. #
City	State/Prov.	Zip/Postal Code

Signature (if under 18, a parent or guardian must sign)

Mail to the **Harlequin Reader Service:**
IN U.S.A.: P.O. Box 1867, Buffalo, NY 14240-1867
IN CANADA: P.O. Box 609, Fort Erie, Ontario L2A 5X3

Not valid to current subscribers of Harlequin Romance books.

**Are you a subscriber of Harlequin Romance books
and want to receive the larger-print edition?
Call 1-800-873-8635 today!**

* Terms and prices subject to change without notice. Prices do not include applicable taxes. Sales tax applicable in N.Y. Canadian residents will be charged applicable provincial taxes and GST. Offer not valid in Quebec. This offer is limited to one order per household. All orders subject to approval. Credit or debit balances in a customer's account(s) may be offset by any other outstanding balance owed by or to the customer. Please allow 4 to 6 weeks for delivery. Offer available while quantities last.

Your Privacy: Harlequin Books is committed to protecting your privacy. Our Privacy Policy is available online at www.eHarlequin.com or upon request from the Reader Service. From time to time we make our lists of customers available to reputable third parties who may have a product or service of interest to you. If you would prefer we not share your name and address, please check here. ☐

HR09R

Coming Next Month

Available July 14, 2009

This summer take a romantic journey round the Mediterranean
or fall in love Stateside with our scorching-hot heroes!
And look out for new author Nina Harrington's first book!

#4105 THE COWBOY'S BABY Patricia Thayer
Baby on Board
Kira and Trace grew apart when they couldn't have children. Now Kira
wants to adopt, and needs her husband's help. Is Trace still the man
who can make Kira's dreams come true?

#4106 THE BROODING FRENCHMAN'S PROPOSAL
Rebecca Winters
Since Laura arrived at his château, Raoul has been certain she's just
another gold digger, but he can't take his eyes off her! Laura wants a
fresh start, but Raoul's searing gaze promises much more....

#4107 THE SICILIAN'S BRIDE Carol Grace
Escape Around the World
If arrogant vintner Dario thinks he can intimidate Isabel into selling
her vineyard, he's got a lot to learn about fiery redheads! His biggest
challenge will be convincing Isabel that all he wants is her!

#4108 HIS L.A. CINDERELLA Trish Wylie
In Her Shoes...
Cassidy can't believe her old flame, Hollywood star Will, is demanding
she honor their old scriptwriting contract, or he'll sue! But even after five
years, their love is still burning....

#4109 DATING THE REBEL TYCOON Ally Blake
As a teenager, Rosie knew gorgeous Cameron was out of her league—
so what's she doing now going on a date with the brooding billionaire?

#4110 ALWAYS THE BRIDESMAID Nina Harrington
Amy has ended up planning her best friend's wedding, with only her
friend's brother's help. But handsome businessman Jared is more than
happy to help sweet, sexy Amy with every last detail!

HRCNMBPA0609